The QUEST for ALHAZRED

The QUEST for ALHAZRED

Donald Tyson

WEIRD HOUSE

Editor & Publisher, Joe Morey
Book design by F. J. Bergmann

ISBN: 978-1-957121-68-0

Weird House Press
Central Point, OR 97502
www.weirdhousepress.com
Join the Weird House mailing list at our website!

Chapter One

My feelings were mixed as I stood in the Lane of Scholars before the green door of my former teacher in the arts of necromancy, Abdul Alhazred. Once I passed through this gateway, I could not in honor turn back. I hesitated and felt a thrill of fear at the base of my spine. Squaring my shoulders, I pulled the chain that rang the brass bell on the other side of the wall.

Alhazred was dead. Of this there could be no doubt. Hundreds of people in the marketplace at Damascus had watched him lifted into the air by an invisible monster and torn apart, the pieces of his body vanishing as they were devoured. They had heard his screams of agony and felt the hot spray of his blood on their upturned faces. That he was dead was certain, but what had become of his remains? Would the monster excrete the bones when it had digested the flesh? If so, on what strange land or in what hidden den would they be deposited?

This was not an abstract question. Alhazred's companion in life, an Egyptian woman named Martala, was determined to search for his corpse, or what was left of it, with the purpose of rendering it down to its essential salts, then reconstituting the necromancer in the flesh. Alhazred had foreseen his fate and Martala's reaction to it. In a letter sent to me shortly before his death, he had asked me to help her in her quest. As his student in the necromantic arts, could I do any less? Yet the prospect chilled my heart. The son of a wealthy trader, I lived a good life in Damascus. Was I really about to cast it aside on the mad whim of an elderly woman I barely knew?

The latch on the other side of the door clattered open to reveal a tall figure in a white cap and white thawb. I recognized the long, solemn face of Alhazred's new manservant, Brunni. His mouth trembled as he looked at me, and I realized the poor man was terrified. Alhazred had hired him only a few days before his death. Recent events must have unnerved him. He glanced left and right along the deserted street, which was already darkened by the gathering shadows of twilight.

I had not expected to see him at the gate. What he had witnessed in this house was more than enough to send most men fleeing after their sanity.

"Is something wrong, Brunni?"

"Have you seen anything, young master?" he said in a hushed tone.

"What do you mean?"

"Anything . . . uncanny."

"Come, Brunni, don't tell me you've seen a ghost?"

He stiffened and drew back without answering. Perhaps he thought I was mocking him. I had no patience to placate the wounded feelings of a servant.

"Inform your mistress, Martala, that Hassid ibn Khaled ibn Umar wishes to converse with her," I said, adopting a formal tone.

He nodded quickly, once more casting a furtive glance up and down the street, then closed the gate. I heard the latch slide into place. I looked uneasily along the Lane of Scholars, wondering what, if anything, had attracted the man's eye.

The narrow cobbled street wound like a serpent between high stone walls, revealing only a small portion of its length. Set in the walls on either side were brightly painted doors of different colors. Behind each door lived a practitioner of forbidden arts. The door next to Alhazred's was painted dark brown. From remarks dropped by my teacher I knew this to be the house of Harkanos, leader of the Council of Mages at Damascus, but I had never seen him nor any of the other wizards who dwelt on the street. It was rumored that they seldom left their houses during the day.

Followers of the Prophet who wished to be recognized as men of good character avoided the Lane of Scholars in the same way they shunned the Street of Harlots. Abdul Alhazred had once done a service for my father. Exactly what that service was, my father had never told me, but when I expressed a wish to him to study the arcane arts, and he found that he could not talk me out of this notion, he had prevailed upon Alhazred to become my teacher. Perhaps he had hoped that a taste of necromancy would arouse a revulsion against it in my breast. If so, he was sorely mistaken. It had determined me to make it my profession.

There was something in the darkening gloom of the deserted street that made me shiver and toy nervously with the end of my beard, which had just recently begun to grow in earnest. I sensed a presence and felt as though I were being watched. With relief I heard the green door rattle open behind me.

"The Mistress will see you now," Brunni said. He cast another nervous glance around as he let me in and secured the latch.

I followed the servant across a spacious courtyard that contained a marble fountain and painted statues of Greek gods and goddesses. Water plashed gently in the fountain. I was fairly certain the water was only a glamour, for how could Alhazred have drawn water up from the ground with such force that it erupted into the air? It was a very good glamour—I felt the coolness of the mist on my face as I passed. The marble fountain itself and the statues I suspected to be real. The wanton poses of the naked goddesses made me blush. Their lapis lazuli and jet-black eyes seemed to follow me.

Brunni escorted me through the brass-clad double doors of the house and along the tiled hall to the library, where he left me with a bow and a silent gesture.

Martala sat at the reading table, a pair of elevated wrought-iron oil lamps burning on either side to supplement the fading daylight. The surface of the table was covered with books and scrolls, some open and others closed. She did not look up from the volume before her when I entered.

I stood watching her for a time. There was a certain nobility in her profile, with its straight nose and high forehead; perhaps a distant echo of the ancient pharaohs of the Nile. Her dark hair, streaked with grey, was pinned up on the back of her head. She wore a light blue Persian tunic. Her dark eyebrows and long eyelashes had no need of kohl, and despite her age her lips retained a natural pink. Her glance up at me revealed her most startling feature, her eyes. They were so pale a shade of blue, they resembled crystals of ice. I knew that in years she was older than my mother, but she looked like a much younger woman.

"Why have you come, Hassid?" she said. "Can't you see that I am busy?"

There was a note of weariness in her voice. I wondered when she had last slept. It was six days after the vanishing of Alhazred from the marketplace. It had taken me that long to put my affairs in order and prepare myself for what I was about to do. Without speaking, I handed her Alhazred's letter.

> *If you are reading this, I am dead, or at least I am assumed to be dead, for I do not believe my corpse will be discovered in Damascus. My enemy knows full well that the body of a man may be reduced to its essential salts and then returned to life and health by the application of an incantation to Yog-Sothoth, who has the power to open all gates, even the gate of death. My companion, Martala, knows the way of this necromancy. It would not be the first time she has used it.*

4

It may seem to you that I have been cold and distant in my manner toward you. Let me tell you now that my feelings for you are not so remote as they seemed. It was my purpose to make necromancy an unattractive subject of study, in order to test the sincerity of your desire, and if possible discourage you from this course of life, which is fraught with danger and sorrow. You remained steadfast in your desire to master the art, and I believe you are sincere.

Therefore, I send you this letter to ask a service of you, which you may freely decline. I know that my companion will seek to find the resting place of my body, so that she may recover it and rend it down to its essential salts. I ask that you help her in this quest.

She is alone in the world. Her determination is iron, her skills and cunning are formidable, but the forces that conspire against her purpose are many and great in power. Become her assistant. She will try to send you away. Do not allow her to do so, but show her this letter and tell her it is my wish that she allow you to help her. It is my belief that your help may prove crucial in the success or failure of her quest.

I will not lie to you, Hassid. I am asking you to leave the security and wealth of your family to venture into forbidden realms where death, and far worse than death, may lurk in every shadow. If you decline, I ask that you burn this letter and say nothing to Martala or anyone else about its contents.

Whatever is your decision, you are a fine young man of good character, with an excellent mind that always seeks the truth. You have my best wishes for your future life, wherever it may lead you.

She read it slowly, folded it and stared across the shadowy library with unfocused eyes, then read it again, blinking rapidly. I realized she was fighting back tears.

"I am here to offer myself to you for whatever use I may be in your quest to recover the remains of Alhazred."

"Why?"

Her question made me pause. "He was my teacher."

"You were only his student for twelve days."

"Twelve lifetimes."

She regarded me for several moments in silence.

"You are barely more than a boy. What use do you think you can be?"

"I have been trained to the sword," I said quickly. "I can read and write, and through my father's business dealings I have established contacts throughout Egypt and Arabia. I know several languages including Persian and Greek. I have wealth—"

"There is no shortage of gold and silver in this house," she said.

"You cannot go alone. You will need a man to speak for you, and to guard your back."

"So you mean to be my bodyguard?" The thought seemed to amuse her. A faint smile played at the corners of her mouth.

I drew my sword and dropped to one knee, holding the straight steel blade naked across my hands.

"I pledge my sword to you, and to my master Abdul Alhazred."

"Get up, get up, you idiot." She shook her head. "Since it was Alhazred's wish that you accompany me, I have no choice but to accept your offer of service. But before you commit yourself, child, know this—you will almost certainly be walking to your own death. Do you understand this?"

"I understand," I said, awkwardly sheathing my sword. "You will have no reason to doubt my courage."

"Take him," a deep gravelly voice said from a corner of the library that was shrouded in shadows.

I looked and saw nothing, then looked again. Eyes glowed against the darkness, and teeth gleamed dimly. A creature of nightmare stepped forward into the lamplight.

Chapter Two

"**W**hat brings you to this house, Uto?" Martala said calmly without rising.

I fumbled for the hilt of my sword and drew it with a rasp of steel against the brass guard on its sheath. The monster crouched and flexed its enormous hands, the fingers of which were tipped with black claws.

"Put your sword away, fool. This is Uto, leader of the White Skull Clan, a friend to Alhazred, and I hope to me as well."

Uto made a kind of coughing sound in his throat that I realized must be his version of laughter.

"You are a ghoul," I said. The descriptions of ghouls I had read since childhood flooded back into my mind. This creature was not quite like any of them. The black velvet of his skin reflected no light and made him almost invisible in the shadows. His body was human-like, but his arms were longer and more muscular than those of a man, and his posture resembled more that of a great ape. His thick neck supported a head with canine attributes. When he spoke, black fangs reflected the lamplight. Small tufts of hair grew from the tips of his pointed ears. He was completely naked save for a belt around his waist and a necklace of beads. He carried no weapon, but with such claws and fangs, he scarcely needed any.

"Are you in the habit of creeping through my house uninvited, Uto?"

The ghoul shrugged his massive shoulders. "I did not want to frighten your servants, so I emerged from your cellar unannounced."

During the course of my studies with Alhazred I had speculated more than once that the cellar might contain access to a tunnel. Here was confirmation.

"How much have you heard?"

"I entered shortly after the boy."

"You move very quietly."

"Thank you for the compliment."

"Why are you here, Uto?"

The creature hesitated, then spoke in a somewhat softer voice. "Alhazred was my friend, and a ghoul of the Black Spring Clan; an adopted ghoul, yes, but still a ghoul. I came to offer my help in honor of his memory. I cannot leave Damascus due to my obligation to my own clan, but any information or service I can provide is yours for the asking."

Martala did not immediately answer. I saw that the ghoul's words had touched her heart.

"I thank you, Uto of the White Skull Clan. I accept your offer of help."

"Good. Now what are we going to do?"

"It is my intention to locate Alhazred's remains and restore him to life from his essential salts." She said it simply, as though it were an easy matter.

"But Alhazred was eaten alive. What is there to find?"

"His essential salts will pass through the demon unaltered. We need only locate its droppings."

The ghoul glanced at me, and then returned his gaze to her. "You intend to go on a quest to find the excrement of a demon?"

She nodded. Uto was silent for a long moment. Then he began to laugh by making that choked sound in his throat. He doubled over, laughing. It was some time before he was able to compose himself.

"Alhazred would have relished this joke," he said.

"Yes," she said with the shadow of a smile.

"How do you intend to proceed?"

"I have been searching through the library for information concerning the demon that consumed him in the marketplace. But I have found nothing useful."

"Do you have any idea why Alhazred was attacked?"

"No. He had been carrying out a private course of study over the past month but he never spoke to me about it, so I do not know what it entailed."

"Have you tried to contact Alhazred's father?" Uto asked.

"His father is still alive?" I said in surprise. Alhazred had appeared to me too advanced in age to have a living parent. Both ignored me.

"I have tried with ink, with oil, with water, and with the stone of Merlinus that Harkanos gave to Alhazred, but Salaymorlaynah does not answer."

"Perhaps he has not learned yet of Alhazred's murder?"

"I find that hard to believe. He is a djinn of the Ninth Circle."

"Alhazred's father is a djinn?" I said. It was as if I were not in the room.

"Speaking of the djinn," Uto said, "what do you intend to do about this little one?" He pointed with his chin at the window behind her. The shutters were still open. I looked but saw nothing, then looked again. There was a faint luminosity beyond the sill against the darkness. It flickered faintly, revealing a countenance out of nightmare.

"It's Sashi, Alhazred's companion," Martala said without surprise. "I wondered what had become of her."

"I did not know these carrion eaters could make themselves visible to human sight," Uto said with amusement.

"It's a trick Alhazred taught to her. Burnni must have glimpsed her lurking outside the house. That's why he's been so nervous lately."

"What is this thing?" I asked.

Something in my voice made Martala glance at me, "A lesser species of djinn known as the *chaklah'i*. Alhazred

9

encountered her while wandering alone in the Empty Space, and formed a bond with her."

"Why doesn't she come in?" Uto asked.

"This house is guarded with powerful wards of magic designed to exclude uninvited visitors. Now that she is separated from Alhazred's body, they must be keeping her out."

She made a gesture with her hand and muttered under her breath. The spectral djinn crawled through the window into the library. I could see only her outline, which flickered with occasional flashes of faint blue fire. It was enough to show a round head with enormous black eyes, a wide mouth full of needle-sharp teeth that seemed to grin, and large erect ears like those of a bat. In surprising contrast, the hands of the djinn were slender and feminine. She made a placating gesture toward Martala.

"I think she wants to come with you on your quest," Uto said.

Martala shook her head. "She would starve. She derives nourishment from the remnants of vitality in corpses."

"They are vermin to my kind," Uto said. "They flock around us when we feed."

"While inside Alhazred, she drew nourishment from his body."

"Perhaps she wants you to carry her."

The djinn shook her head vigorously and pointed at me. Uto coughed laughter.

"It seems she wishes the boy to carry her."

"I don't understand," I said. "You mean carry her on my back?"

Martala regarded me seriously. "Sashi does you a great honor. I don't know why she chose you, but perhaps there is more to you than I had assumed. Will you carry her?"

"I suppose I could rig up some kind of backpack."

Again the ghoul laughed. I found my annoyance rising.

"Tell Sashi you will carry her," Martala said.

I turned to the faintly glimmering creature. "I will bear you with me, if that is what you wish. It will be an honor to have the companion of Alhazred as my companion."

The djinn rushed toward me. Before I could move she was all around me, pressing inward. I felt her insubstantial body slide into my chest and touch my heart and other organs with coolness, then spread itself along my limbs and into my head. I staggered and almost fell, not from pain, for there was none, but from sheer surprise.

The face of a beautiful young woman with large amber eyes floated in the air before me.

I thank you for accepting me, Hassid, she said in a mellow voice that did not seem to come to my ears from the air, but to be in my mind.

"It is little enough to do for my master," I said aloud.

"She is seated within him," Martala said.

"You humans are a strange race," Uto said, shaking his massive black head. "No ghoul would tolerate such a violation."

"She can speak through Hassid," Martala said. "Tell us, Sashi, what happened in the marketplace?"

I echoed the djinn's words aloud as she spoke them to me.

"It came without warning, an invisible demon of the air. One moment there was nothing, and then it had my beloved in its grasp. He had no chance to draw his sword, although I do not believe it would have helped him to do so. Before he could even cry out, it tore him in half. I was cast out from his body. I fought against it, but I do not believe it even noticed my presence. Holding my beloved with its many limbs, it ripped away his arms and legs and began to devour them."

Tears streamed down the cheeks of the face floating in my mind. I felt the chillness of her pain in my heart.

"That is as I remember," Martala said without emotion. "Did you recognize the kind of demon it was?"

"It was not one I have ever before encountered. I can only say that it felt alien to me, as though it were not entirely of this world."

11

Martala rummaged across the table, pushing the books and scrolls aside, until she found a clear crystal globe that was around the size and shape of a large hen's egg.

"It that what I think it is?" Uto asked.

"The stone of Merlinus," she said. "It will not open for me, but perhaps Harkanos can use it to reach Salaymorlaynah."

"Good," Uto said. "Let us go to him now."

Chapter Three

"I was filled with sorrow to learn of Alhazred's death. Not only was he my friend, but it is a great loss to the Council of Mages."

The speaker was a tall man with a clean-shaven face and curling light-brown hair that was cut short to expose his ears. His complexion and profile suggested Greek origins, but he spoke with no trace of accent. His eyes were a clear grey that seemed to penetrate to the depths of my soul when he looked at me, which wasn't often. He wore an ivory-colored silk robe with golden embroidery; and around his neck a curious silver pendant in the shape of an inverted crescent moon with seed pearls dangling from its points. I could not determine his age. At some moments he appeared a man of no more than thirty years, but at other moments, when the light from the lamp struck his face from a different angle, he seemed much older.

The room was dimly lit by a single oil lamp that hung from an iron bracket on the wall. I sat with Martala on a divan. Uto crouched on his heels in the corner, away from the light, silent and almost invisible. He had declined to take a chair when it had been offered.

The tall man, whom I took to be the mage Harkanos, master of the house, settled himself into a chair opposite us while a slender young woman in a green silk dress poured white wine from a decanter into crystal cups on the low table. She withdrew to a sideboard with the vessel.

"I would not have troubled you, Harkanos, but I know of no other mage I can trust," Martala said.

"You intend to search for the remains of Alhazred and reconstitute him from his essential salts."

"That is my intention."

"And your companions, will they help you to accomplish your purpose?"

"The boy goes with me. Uto cannot leave Damascus."

He studied me with a serious expression. I felt myself being evaluated and wondered what his conclusion might be, but his face did not change.

"A pity Altrus is no longer with us."

"It was a great loss."

The name was unfamiliar to me, but it did not seem my place to speak, so I remained silent.

"How is his family?"

"His wife, Nealayna, and his children have their own house not far from the palace of the Caliph. Altrus left them well provided for."

"He did not wish to be reanimated?"

"No, it was his desire to have a natural death."

"Alhazred possessed wealth. You should use it to hire mercenaries."

"I want to move swiftly and unnoticed. A fighting force would only slow me down." She hesitated. "Besides, who can I trust?"

"Have you determined the identity of your foe?"

She shook her head. "That is why I came to you."

"Do you think it is . . . the one who should not be named?"

"I don't know."

"Alhazred spoke to me of him several times," Uto said. "He believed the Crawling Chaos hated him and wished to torment and to kill him."

"What can a woman and a boy do against such a powerful enemy?" Harkanos mused aloud, shaking his head.

"We don't know who sent the demon to consume Alhazred, or why," she reminded him. "Alhazred had many enemies." She drew from her pocket the crystal globe. It gleamed coldly in the lamplight, its color similar to that of her eyes.

"The stone of Merlinus," he said. "Have you looked into it?"

"I tried to use it to contact Alhazred's father, but the stone will not open for me."

"That is probably because your emotions are disturbed. This matter lies close to your heart. To work the stone requires tranquility of mind."

"It is my hope that you will attempt to reach Salaymor-laynah on my behalf," she said.

"I shall make the attempt." He took the stone from her and cradled it in his lap between his hands, gazing down at it. We waited and watched. The minutes passed.

At last he shrugged his shoulders and raised his head.

"There is some kind of ward across the crystal that prevents me from opening it."

"That is what I felt," Martala said. "It is almost as though some force is holding the stone shut."

"Let me try, Father," the girl at the sideboard said.

I had forgotten she was in the room, so quietly had she stood listening.

"That would not be wise, Anisah. Your mind is too delicate."

"If your daughter can open the crystal you must let her try," Martala said.

"There is a power behind the ward," he said. "I did not like the way it tasted."

"She is no longer a naked child," Uto put in with his rough voice. "She is a woman who can choose her own path."

"I will decide what path my daughter walks," Harkanos said sharply. Silence held the room for a dozen heartbeats.

"No, Father, you must let me decide," Anisah told him gently. "The life of Alhazred hangs in the balance. If I can be of help, you must allow it."

The mage sat brooding, turning the crystal between his hands. I could see that his friendship for Alhazred warred with his concern for his daughter's well-being.

"If I allow you to look into the stone, you must alert me at the first sign of danger. Do you understand? Danger of any kind."

"Of course, Father."

He passed the stone to her reluctantly. She sat beside his chair on the rug with her legs crossed beneath her long dress and cradled the crystal in her hands.

"It's so cold," she said.

No one spoke.

"I see how it is," she murmured. "The lock is a puzzle. Its key is a symbol held in the mind. Let me play with it for a time."

She began to hum softly to herself. Her voice was clear and musical. I studied her bowed head. Her golden hair hung loosely over her shoulders. Her complexion was unusually pale. In that respect it was very similar to the complexion of Alhazred, about whom it was rumored that he never tanned no matter how much time he spent under the sun. Her nose was straight, her lips full but pale, her chin firm. She was quite beautiful. I wondered where her mother might be. Was she sleeping in a room above, or had she passed from this life?

"There, I have it," she said. "The crystal opens."

"Call out to Salaymorlaynah," Martala said eagerly. "Tell him that his son, Alhazred, urgently needs his help."

"I see him," she said. "He stands before a fireplace. His back is to me. Now he turns."

With a faint cry, she dropped the stone. It rolled across the rug. Uto straightened from his crouch and picked it up. Harkanos had dropped to one knee from his chair to comfort his daughter in his arms.

"He thrust me away. I am not hurt, Father, but he was very rude."

Before Harkanos could reply, the air began to stir. It swirled

16

more strongly, making the flame of the oil lamp flutter and almost go out. Suddenly, there was a man standing in the room. Tall, with a dignified bearing, he wore a Roman toga in the style of the patricians of that city centuries ago. His hair was dusky blond, his face clean-shaven, his eyes the color of green jade—the same color as the eyes of Alhazred. The air of the room ceased to eddy.

"I am not here," he said in a mellow voice.

"I understand," Harkanos said.

"Well, I do not," Uto said. "Who are you?"

"I am Salaymorlaynah, a djinn of the Ninth Circle and Alhazred's father."

"You came," Anisah said with delight.

"I could scarcely ignore your collective importunities any longer." There was humor in his voice.

"I take it you are forbidden to act?"

"You have always been perceptive, Harkanos. I am compelled, in ways that I will not attempt to describe, to avoid any effort to discover the fate of my son, or to act against his enemies."

"You must tell us where his remains lie, so that we can retrieve them," Martala said with passion.

"That I do not know, nor the identity of his enemy. I have heard only rumors concerning his death, mutterings in deep, dark places by things that are not human."

"What do they mutter?" Uto demanded.

"They say Alhazred was meddling in matters he would have done better to avoid." Salaymorlaynah looked at Martala. "Does that mean anything to you?"

"Nothing. For the past month or so he has been entirely engaged in research having to do with his art. He had little time for anything else, other than instructing Hassid, which he undertook as an obligation to a friend."

"What was the nature of this research?"

"That I do not know for certain," she admitted. "He did not speak about it. I only know that he was sending out sprites to acquire information."

"Sprites?" Uto asked.

"Spiritual servants with mercurial properties, useful in matters involving research into arcane subjects," Harkanos said.

"His research may have involved alchemy," Martala said. "One time I chanced to see some notes he was making, and they appeared alchemical. But I cannot imagine why this study would be the cause of his death."

Harkanos turned to me. "While Alhazred was instructing you, did he say anything or do anything that might have bearing on his demise?"

I thought for several seconds, than shook my head.

"It is possible that Alhazred's alchemical probings awoke the ire of some powerful mage," Harkanos said to the djinn.

"He provoked the anger of someone having considerably greater power than any mage."

"You mean a god?"

"Or a being of similar potency."

The silence lengthened. A thought occurred to me. I hesitated to voice it in such daunting company, but at last could not resist. "Is it possible the djinn that was inside Alhazred at the time of his death knows anything that might be of value?"

"Ask her," Martala said.

Sashi's face appeared before my sight when I closed my eyes. *Do you have any information to offer?* I thought.

She spoke in my mind, and I repeated her words aloud for the others.

"I did not understand the study Alhazred was engaged in, but there were two place names that of late were often in his thoughts. One of them was Soumela."

"The name means nothing to me," Harkanos said.

"It is supposed to be Christian monastery some distance beyond Cappadocia," Salaymorlaynah said.

"Why, supposed to be?" Martala asked.

"Because the monks, who pretend to be Christians, engage in the study of the black arts, alchemy chief among them. It is whispered that they worship Yog-Sothoth."

"The *chaklah* spoke of two places," Uto said. "What is the other?"

When Sashi spoke the name, a shiver of dread passed through my body. My face must have gone pale, for the others regarded me strangely.

"Leng," I said, my voice choking on the word.

"That foul place," Martala said. "I know it."

"You have been to Leng?" Harkanos asked in surprise.

"With Alhazred. It is not a part of the world I would care to revisit. If, indeed, it may even be said to be in this world."

Sashi spoke again in my mind unbidden. I repeated her words aloud. "There was something else—a strange word often in his thoughts. Shenghuo."

Martala looked at Harkanos.

"It means nothing to me," he said with a shake of his head.

"Permit me to enlighten you," Salaymorlaynah told him. "There is a great house of black stone on the northern part of the Plateau of Leng that is little known and universally avoided by those who have heard of it. It is inhabited by a sect of fanatics that had its origin in the eastern extremity of the world, in the land of Chin. They call themselves Shenghuo."

"What interest can this sect hold for us?" she asked.

"It is said that the men who occupy this house practice arts that originated in the Black Land."

"Egypt, you mean."

The djinn nodded.

"It is called the Black Land due to the color of the rich soil along the banks of the Nile," Martala explained to Anisah.

"What are these arts?" Uto asked.

"Alchemy. Chief among them is the making of gold from baser metals, but they also involve the making of jewels, and the removal or concealing of flaws in gems to increase their value."

"This makes no sense," Martala said with a shake of her head. "Alhazred had no want of gold or jewels."

"Some alchemists also seek to perfect themselves by refining all gross qualities from their minds and all weaknesses from their bodies," Salaymorlaynah said. "They call this their Great Work. Is it possible my son sought to perfect himself?"

"That is more likely," Martala said. "Alhazred was always seeking to better himself. Perhaps in alchemy he thought he had found a way to restore his face."

"That is possible," Harkanos agreed. "Although he did not speak of it, I sensed that his facial disfigurement troubled him."

"I don't understand," I said. "There was nothing wrong with Alhazred's face."

The others regarded me in silence. I felt that I had spoken the words of a fool.

"How did Alhazred appear to you?" Martala asked gently.

"As a handsome man of mature years, although he moved like a younger man."

"You did not see his face," Uto said.

"That's absurd," I protested. "I saw his face every day of my studies."

"What you saw was a glamour that Alhazred used as a mask to conceal his mutilated features. In his youth, he was disfigured by the late King Huban of Sana'a in Yemen as punishment for deflowering the king's only daughter."

"What kind of mutilations?"

"His nose was cut off, and his ears. His cheeks were slashed open and deeply scarred." She hesitated. "The king did . . . other things to Alhazred that were concealed by his clothing."

I felt sick. How could I have failed to see such damage to my teacher's face?

"He always seemed to me a handsome man, for his advanced age."

Uto laughed. "How old did he look to you?"

"Perhaps seventy-five years, perhaps a bit younger."

"Alhazred was the son of a djinn," Harkanos said. "Such

progeny do not show their age, and are very long of life. You saw what Alhazred wished you to see, that is all."

"He aged his glamour so that his face would match his years of life," Martala explained. "He did not wish people to know that he was almost immortal."

"What will you do now?" Harkanos asked her.

She shrugged. "What can I do? I have only one course open to me. I must journey to this monastery of Soumela and ask these monks if they know anything about Alhazred's death."

"What of Leng?" Salaymorlaynah asked.

"I do not know how to reach it. The Plateau of Leng is not wholly of this world."

"The monks of Soumela may be able to help you, if they are so inclined. They are reputed to be the masters of gateways. Yog-Sothoth favors them because of their worship and the sacrifices they offer up to him."

"You have a long and weary road ahead of you if you plan to ride beyond Cappadocia," Uto said. "All for what may be a fool's errand."

"It is a faint hope," Martala agreed in a quiet voice. "But faint is better than none."

The room fell silent as we brooded on the future. After a time, Anisah stood.

"I will go with you," she said to Martala.

Chapter Four

"Daughter, you cannot leave this house." The tone of Harkanos was grave. "You know the reason."

She confronted her father defiantly, her hands closed into fists. "I have stayed hidden here for too long, Father. I am tired of hiding. I want to go out into the world and see some of it."

"It is too dangerous," Martala said.

"When I was abducted by the black monks, it was Alhazred and you who came to rescue me."

"A rescue that resulted in your death," Martala reminded her.

"But you tried. You both risked your lives for mine. Can I do less for you?"

"We do not need you to sacrifice your life for ours."

This talk was bewildering to me. The girl seemed very much alive. "Who are these black monks?" I asked.

"A gnostic sect of devil worshipers," Uto said. "They wear black robes."

Martala took the hands of the girl into hers. "If Alhazred were here, he would tell you to stay at home with your father."

"I am not helpless," Anisah said. "Since my father resurrected me from my essential salts twelve years ago, I have come to recognize certain abilities inherent in the bloodline of my mother, who as you know was a queen of faerie on the western isle of Albion. I may prove of more use to you than you imagine."

"Will the black monks know if she leaves your house?" Uto asked.

"They will know," Harkanos said. "As long as she remained reduced to her essential salts, they had no interest in this house. I thought after the passage of decades they had forgotten about her, but somehow they learned of her reconstitution twelve years ago, and their agents have never ceased to watch and wait for her to step forth beyond the occult wards around these walls that prevent their entry."

"They must be powerful mages for you to fear them so," Uto said.

"It is not so much them I fear, but the foul gods they worship. They are under the protection of powerful entities, with whom they have made pacts, or I would have destroyed them years ago." He turned to his daughter. "You are of age, Anisah. I cannot forbid you to do this thing, but if you leave this house I can no longer watch over you."

She came forward and bowed her head to kiss him on the cheek. "You have protected me all my life, Father. At some point, a baby bird must try its wings."

"You speak the truth," he admitted.

"We will ride fast from the gate of Damascus," she said, excitement in her voice. "The black monks will not be able to catch us, even if by some dark magic they learn of our purpose."

"It is a very long journey, my child."

"As to that," Salaymorlaynah said, "I may be able to help you. But remember, I am not here. You have not seen me."

He stepped to the open floor and made a gesture. The air sparkled for an instant.

Upon the floor lay a woven rug. It appeared to me to be a prayer rug of some kind, although it was slightly larger than is usual for its kind, and the design woven into it was strange. It had been well used over many years, whatever its function. The colors dyed into its wool were faded, and in places the warp and weft of the backing was visible through the thinness of the nap.

I studied its pattern in the dim lamplight. It was geometric, but unlike any geometry I had ever seen. The interlocking spirals woven into it bewildered my eyes and frustrated my attempts to trace them.

"Is that what I think it is?" The words escaped my mouth before I could stop them.

"Yes, and no, young Hassid," Salaymorlaynah said with a smile.

"Enough riddles," Uto said in irritation. "What is this thing?"

"Have you ever heard tales of flying carpets?"

Uto made a sound of choked laughter in his throat. "I have heard of such things spoken about in stories told to human children by their grandmothers as they are being put into bed."

"They are real enough, though few in number," the djinn said. "But the stories about them told to children are not quite accurate."

Uto reached down to touch the carpet.

"No," Salaymorlaynah said in a quiet voice that stopped his hand in midair, than added, "that would be unwise."

"You have bound a spirit of the air into it," Harkanos said with understanding.

"I did not make it. I merely borrowed it for your use. With luck, I will be able to return it before its owner realizes it was gone."

"Do the djinn need luck?" Uto said.

"Everyone needs luck, even the gods."

"How is it to be controlled?" Harkanos asked.

"It feeds on wine, tears and blood. It is fearful of fire and of cold iron. When commanded with its name to carry you to a place, it cannot refuse, but it will not do so willingly. It resents its bondage."

"How do I communicate with it?" Martala asked.

"Concentrate your thoughts. The name of the spirit woven into it is Ly'saqua. By knowing its name you now have power over it."

"I understand."

"Use your rod on it if it tries to disobey you, but have a care lest you destroy the weave and release the spirit into the air, for then its wrath will be great against you."

I could not prevent a laugh of disbelief escaping my lips. "Do you mean we should all stand together upon that little thing, and it will carry us through the air to Cappadocia?"

"In a manner of speaking," Salaymorlaynah said.

"Will it carry me to Leng?" Martala asked him.

"No. It is a creature of the airy elemental zone that rings our world. It cannot pass through the higher portals of Yog-Sothoth."

"Is it very dangerous?" I could not refrain from the question, given the caution Harkanos had spoken to the ghoul.

"It will kill you if it gets a chance, young Hassid," Salaymorlaynah said. "So do not give it the opportunity."

"When will you use it?" Harkanos asked Martala.

"In the morning. We must prepare ourselves for a long journey, even if we are to be carried above the mountains. It is a pity the carpet is too small to accommodate horses or camels."

"I will come to your house on the morrow, after I make my own preparations for the journey," Anisah said.

"Pack all you will need to survive so you can carry it on your shoulders," Martala told her. "Food, water, a sleeping roll, a blanket, and an extra garment. Wear boots on your feet. I suggest you dress like a man in a Persian tunic and pants. I have found that to be the most serviceable clothing for long journeys."

"Should I hide my hair and pretend to be a boy?"

Martala eyed her womanly body up and down. "I don't believe that would be of use. The curve of your hips and the swell of your breasts are too evident. You will travel as

26

my servant, along with Hassid. I will go in the guise of a wealthy Egyptian woman of social standing who is seeking to learn the forbidden arts of alchemy, and is willing to pay well for instruction. A pity gold is so heavy—we can only each carry a small number of coins."

Martala bent to roll up the carpet.

"Carefully," Salaymorlaynah said.

It rippled as she touched its hem and seemed to squirm like the body of a snake. She grasped it and rolled it tightly. Four strips of cloth hung from its ends wherewith it could be tied closed. She knotted them and picked it up, placing it under her arm.

"There is no more I can do to help you," Salaymorlaynah said. "I could not even do this much, for I was never here. None of you have spoken to me."

"Thank you for your help," Martala told him.

But she spoke to the empty air, for Salaymorlaynah was gone.

Chapter Five

"Don't crowd, Hassid, you're pushing me off the edge," Martala snapped in irritation.

I inched closer to the center of the carpet. The packs of provisions we wore on our shoulders made it awkward to stand together on its small surface. Late morning sunlight shone over the wall into the courtyard of Alhazred's house. From the fruit trees in the back I heard birds singing. Martala had spread the carpet out on the paving stones beside the fountain. I felt Anisah's back parts press against the front of my thighs and cringed away from her, not wishing to dishonor her. This caused me to again bump into Martala behind me.

"Dolt," she said.

Brunni stood a few steps away, watching respectfully with his long, solemn face, his arms folded on his chest. What he made of our bizarre performance I could only imagine.

"Prepare yourselves," Martala said. She paused, and said in a deeper voice, "Ly'saqua, I command you to carry us to the monastery of Soumela."

I braced my feet and gently held onto Anisah's pack, which was close to my face. We waited. Nothing happened.

"Ly'saqua, you cannot defy me," Martala said with an edge in her tone. "I know your true name. Carry us to Soumela."

I looked aside at Brunni. His eyes met mine but his expression did not change.

"I command you, Ly'saqua, lift us into the air."

Martala stomped her boot on the carpet. She began to curse in Egyptian. At least, I assume they were curses. They were words with which I was unfamiliar. After some minutes of this pantomime, which must have greatly entertained Brunni although he did not show it, Martala stepped off the carpet.

"Get off," she said.

We stepped from the wool to the paving stones. Without another word she tramped into the house. After a short while she emerged with a bamboo carpet beater in her hand. She began to beat the surface of the carpet, which caused dust to arise from its well-worn nap.

"You will obey me, Ly'saqua, or I will make you wish you had never been spawned."

I looked at Anisah. She shook her head. As Martala had suggested the previous night, she had worn a tunic and pants. Strong leather travel boots were laced to her feet. Her head was covered with a white mantel but her face was unveiled, and golden curls escaped from under the garment. I marveled at her beauty. Her countenance glowed in the morning light as if with some inner radiance.

"Hassid, stop making cow eyes at Anisah and take this beater. My arm is tired."

Wordlessly I accepted the carpet beater from Martala and began to strike the carpet. If nothing else, I thought, it would be free of dust by the end of this futile exercise.

"Perhaps there is another way," Anisah said.

I stopped with my arm raised.

"Salaymorlaynah said something about nourishment."

"You think I should feed it?" Martala asked.

Anisah spread her hands silently.

"Brunni, bring a cup of red wine," Martala told the servant, who hurried into the house. He soon returned with a wooden cup filled with red wine.

Taking the cup, Martala poured it over the carpet. I expected the nap to be stained red, but the wine was somehow absorbed into the wool without leaving a stain or any sign of wetness. The carpet rippled as though a strong gust of wind had blown across it.

"Quick, get on," Martala said.

I waited for Anisah to position herself as before and crowded in behind her. The Egyptian woman pressed against my back. Her arms encircled my waist.

"Hold onto Anisah," she said. "If you let her fall I will gut you alive."

I hesitated, but saw the wisdom of her words. Gingerly, I slid my hands around the girl's slender waist. She did not object.

"Now, Ly'saqua, carry us to Soumela."

I braced myself for the carpet to rise beneath my feet. Instead, the air began to swirl around us. It was as if we stood in the center of a dust devil. The air swirled faster and faster, and began to sparkle. Sparks of all colors appeared: green, blue, orange, violet, red. I blinked the dust from my eyes, and saw the courtyard beyond the wall of swirling wind begin to turn, as though it too had become caught up in the vortex. The shape of Brunni slid past, then the fountain, then the front door of the house with its framing marble pillars. Again and again they passed, and strangely as I watched they began to blur and run together like colored paints poured and stirred in a vessel of oil. Soon the images were gone, and only the streaks of color remained, spinning around us at ever increasing speed. The roar of the wind in our ears made it impossible to hear anything else. I felt Martala's hands tighten around my waist, and I tightened my own around the waist of the girl.

Then, as quickly as it had begun, it was over. I blinked several times and looked around. We stood in the open on rocky ground. A few bushes grew from between the rocks. Before us reared the steep side of a mountain. The air felt strange. I realized its temperature had changed, and it had a different smell. The sun was higher in the sky, which was to be expected—Cappadocia lay further eastward from Damascus.

The carpet rippled and rolled beneath our feet. I felt its hem brush my leg with woolly fingers.

"Get off it," Martala said.

Stepping quickly to the bare ground, I drew Anisah with me, having a care that she did not stumble. We stood together, watching the undulating carpet.

"I think it's still hungry," I said.

"It can stay that way until we next have need of it," Martala said.

She reached down and firmly grasped the edge. The carpet fought against her touch like a living thing, but she rolled it tightly and held it rolled with her knee while she knotted its ties.

"It didn't take us to the monastery," Anisah said.

I pointed up at the mountain. "Can that be it up there?"

Partway up the mountainside windows had been cut into the rock, and there were terraces.

"It must be," Martala said.

"Why didn't the carpet bear us inside it?" the girl asked.

"Maybe the monastery has some kind of ward around it to keep out enemies, like the wards around your father's house, and Alhazred's."

I noted that Martala had not said "my house." Alhazred was not yet dead to her.

"We have a long climb," I said.

There was a path of sorts, narrow and little used. We began to climb the slope, following it as it wound its way up the mountainside. At length we came to a simple but ancient wooden door. It opened of its own accord before I could pound on it with my fist. Our presence had been noted by those within the monastery. I wondered if the unconventional manner of our arrival in the valley below had also been observed from this eagle's nest.

A young man with a shaved head, who wore a simple monk's cassock of snow-white wool that was devoid of adornment, regarded us impassively.

"I am a pilgrim," Martala said in Greek. "The fame of

Soumela Monastery compelled me to present myself at your gate. I ask for an audience with your abbot."

"What would be your name?" he asked.

"I am the Lady Cassandra Cassilia Pakali, of late a resident of the city of Alexandria in Egypt, and a seeker of wisdom and truth."

I marvelled at the way the name rolled from her lips and wondered if she had composed it in her head beforehand.

"And these?"

"This is my bodyguard, Hassid, and my handmaiden Douli. They go with me everywhere."

The monk looked at me for a moment, then at the girl. He blinked slowly. "The Abbot Nicodemus does not give audiences to travelers."

"I have no doubt his time is very valuable. I am willing to pay for it with gold."

She drew forth her purse and opened it, letting a few gold dinars fall onto her palm. She kept one and poured the rest back.

"Perhaps this will compensate you for your trouble?"

He hesitated, then took the coin and opened the door wider. "Come into the courtyard and wait. I will speak to the Abbot."

The sight of the monastery had been concealed from clear view on the ascent up the path. For the first time I was able to see it all. It was cut into the side of the mountain, as so many Christian monasteries are, and protected from the weather by an overhang of rock, but what distinguished it were the numerous colorful paintings that adorned its walls. Dozens of serious faces stared back at me, most of them men, but there were a few portraits of women as well. They were everywhere, on every exposed flat surface.

"It's as if a hundred mad painters had been given brushes and let loose in this place," Martala murmured.

"They must be portraits of Christian saints," Anisah said.

A group of three white-robed monks who passed us in the courtyard with their hands hidden in their sleeves eyed us in a guarded way. Others who walked along a pillared gallery that overlooked where we stood gazed down and murmured amongst themselves. I could not hear their words, but I did not like their sly sidelong glances.

The young monk who had opened the gateway returned at a measured pace with his hands clasped in front of his groin.

"The Abbot Nicodemus will see the Lady Pakali," he said. "Please follow me. My name is Cyril, and I have been assigned to care for your needs."

Chapter Six

The monk led us up a set of stone steps and under the looming curtain of the cliff, then along the gallery I had observed earlier and into the inner halls of the monastery, finally stopping before a door that was covered in red leather held in place by large brass nails.

"The Abbot Nicodemus will receive you now." He lifted the latch and opened the door. We started forward.

"Not your servants," he said in startled surprise.

"But my servants are almost a part of me. We go everywhere together. They are seekers of truth, even as am I," Martala told him with a smile.

He hesitated.

A deep voice from the room beyond boomed out. "Let them all come in, Brother Cyril. We won't stand on ceremony."

The monk edged aside. We filed into the spacious room, which was lightened by two large windows cut into the exterior face of the cliff, the shutters of which were thrown wide. A fireplace had been hollowed out of the rock on one side. The morning air was mild, and no fire burned on its grate. In the middle of the room stood a massive desk of dark wood surrounded by several chairs of simple design. The other side of the room was occupied by shelves of books and scrolls. It was an impressive library for so remote a monastery. There must have been several hundred works.

A large man in a robe the color of freshly spilled blood

stood from behind the desk and rounded it, moving with surprising balance and swiftness given his bulk, which was equal to that of two ordinary men. Nor was it all fat. I am not wanting in height, but his head, shrouded beneath a simple cap of red linen that hung down in the back, towered over mine by at least two hands. He was almost a giant. The lower half of his broad face was obscured by a full curling beard of reddish-brown color. A golden medallion on a heavy gold chain rested against his chest. Engraved on it I recognized the astrological symbols for the Head and Tail of the Dragon, surrounded by a serpent with its tail held between its jaws.

"Let me relieve you of your burden, Lady Pakali," he said in a voice so deep, I could feel it as well as hear it. His great chest made the words reverberate like the distant thunder of giant drums.

Martala slid her arms out of her pack and allowed him to ease it to the floor. His eyes, which were a smoky blue color, fixed for a moment on the rolled carpet tied to its side before he released the shoulder straps.

"I am surprised a lady of your obvious breeding would carry such a burden."

"I seek to humble myself before God by walking the earth," Martala told him. "I am but a simple woman, no better than these who toil for me."

"An admirable attitude, and so rare in these times of decadent excesses. Please, seat yourself and rest from your long climb."

I glanced at Anisah. We had not been offered chairs. Discreetly, I motioned her to stand against the wall and stood beside her.

"What extraordinary paintings you have in your monastery," Martala said. "I had heard of them, of course, but to see them with my own eyes. This alone has justified my journey, though I hope there is more that may be revealed to me, in time."

"There is a small group of nuns living at Soumela who see to its cleaning and other housekeeping duties," he said with a smile. "Should you wish to join their number I am sure some arrangement can be made."

"That is most generous of you, Abbot, but my purpose is somewhat more arcane, if I may use such a word without offense."

"No offense at all."

She leaned forward in her chair, eying the abbot across his desk with a serious expression. "Soumela is famed far and wide for its studies in the art of the Black Land. For many years I have been a student of this art. I have traveled far and wide, even as far as Constantinople, and studied this art under many masters both in the land of Egypt and Arabia, but I have yet to attain its mastery. And so I come to you today, a humble pilgrim seeking your wisdom, your teachings, your guidance in this art of transformations."

"You speak of alchemy," he said, sitting back in his chair. The smile slipped from his face.

"Yes, alchemy. I seek to perfect in myself the Great Work, and I know of no other master at whose feet I may learn it than the far-famed and greatly admired Abbot of Soumela."

If her flattering words affected him, he did not show it.

"What you ask is impossible," he said, shaking his head. "These studies you speak about are a secret matter that lies at the very heart of our Order, which I'm sure you know is the Order of Ambrose. We are sworn never to divulge these secrets to outsiders."

"I am a wealthy woman. But I have grown weary of the burden of material possessions, and my gold and silver, my gems, my estates in Egypt, mean nothing to me. Surely you can find it in your heart to save the soul of a seeker after truth? I will renounce everything I own and give it to this monastery, nay, directly to you, good Abbot, and will become one of your nuns. It will give me joy to wash the floors of this great monastery and empty its slop buckets, if only I am permitted to sit at your feet and hear your wisdom."

She reached across the desk and took his massive hand

in hers. He stared at her in perplexity, but I could see the wheels revolve inside his skull.

"Estates in Egypt, you say?"

"Thousands of acres of good farmland on the Delta, and several palaces. Alas, they remain closed for most of the year. I have so little use for them."

"And your gold?"

"It is safe in a vault in Alexandria, ready to be released and conveyed here upon the sending of a secret code that I arranged with my banker before leaving that city." She stood up and took out her purse, then emptied the gold it contained onto the top of his desk. She motioned for me and the girl to approach. We dumped out our purses on top of the contents of hers. It made a charming heap of gold coins that could not have been less than five hundred in number.

The Abbot stared at them as through in meditation, then reluctantly broke his gaze from the gold and looked at Martala.

"Please, please, there is no need to display your wealth. Put your coins away. You are the guests of the monastery. You need not pay for anything—all your requirements will be met. As for your request to become one of my pupils, I will give it my consideration, and make a judgment on the morrow."

"May I dare to hope?" Martala asked in a little girl's voice as she scooped a third of the coins back into her purse.

"I can say only this—the door of wisdom is not entirely shut against you."

"You give me great joy. We will not trouble you further at this time, for I see that you are a man with many responsibilities."

The Abbot rang a silver bell that rested on the corner of his desk as Anisah and I approached to retrieve the contents of our purses with bowed heads. The monk Cyril entered. He eyed the last of the coins we gathered from the desk.

"Take up the Lady Pakali's pack and show her to our best guest chamber. See that all her wants are met."

"And those of my servants," Martala said.

"Of course, of course," Nicodemus boomed with an indulgent smile. "Take care of her servants as well."

"My servants will sleep with me," Martala told Cyril when we had left the office of the Abbot.

"Would you not prefer a private room?" he asked.

"No. One room is sufficient for all. But if you can find a fur or a blanket to throw on the floor for them to lie upon, I'm sure they would be grateful."

Cyril nodded and continued along the gallery. We entered a different part of the monastery, which I saw was a building of considerable extent. It not only ran across the face of the mountain, but deep into its heart. As we left the light of day, the corridors were illuminated by oil lamps. Beneath the smoky odor of burning fat, I smelled the faint tang of sulfur. It did not emanate from the lamps, and I wondered about its source.

A white-robed nun passed us with a broom in her hands. She looked shyly at Martala, and I saw that she was a girl no older than Anisah. Her attractive face was marred by a purple bruise on her left cheek. It appears to be of recent acquisition, for her left eye was bloodshot. Cyril pulled her aside and said something to her in a harsh tone about fresh bed linen and sheep skins. She hurried off with her head bowed.

The monk stopped before a door of carved cedar planks held together by wrought-iron hinges. I noted two things— the door was too massive to break, and there was a bolt to seal it shut on its outside. Neither observation comforted me. There was something in the pale-blue eyes of the hearty Abbot, and something in the timid manner of the bruised nun that combined in my heart to feed a burrowing worm of worry.

"My servants and I are hungry after our long walk. Perhaps before we enter our chamber you will show us to your kitchens, where we may feast on some simple but nourishing fare?" Martala said.

"You will dine with us. The early evening meal is announced by the triple striking of a gong," Cyril said.

"How will we hear it so deep inside the mountain?"

"The gong is audible throughout the monastery. But do not concern yourself, Lady Pakali. A nun will be sent to guide you and your servants to the dining hall."

Martala motioned me to take her pack from the monk. He left us inside the room and closed the door. I waited for the sound of the bolt sliding home, but did not hear it. After a few moments, I went to the door and opened it. The lamp-lit corridor was empty.

Martala took her pack from my hand and dropped it on the floor, went to the large bed, and threw herself across it on her back. Anisah slid off her own pack and sat on the edge of the bed beside the feet of the Egyptian women. I looked around the bedchamber.

The room was of no great size, but there was space enough for the bed and a table with several chairs. The stone walls were covered by woven tapestries, except for the wall opposite the bed, which bore the painting of a woman's head and shoulders. A golden halo surrounded her head. She was looking down with a mild expression, a faint smile on her lips. Four lamps attached to the walls by iron brackets were alight, which gave the room more than sufficient illumination.

I wondered who had lit them. Someone must have run from the Abbot's office to the room to perform this task before our arrival, for it could not be that the monastery left lamps burning in unoccupied chambers. But perhaps the chamber had been readied for our use upon our entry into the courtyard.

"What did you think of the Abbot Nicodemus?" Martala asked.

Anisah and I glanced at each other.

"An unusual man," I said.

"Bigger than most," Martala agreed.

"His manner changed when you showed him the gold and spoke about estates in the Delta."

"As I expected. Monasteries such as this survive on the charity of wealthy patrons."

"For someone who claims to know how to make gold, his monastery seems strangely lacking in opulence."

"I agree," Martala said.

"I do not like him," Anisah said in a quiet voice. "There are snakes in his skull, eating at his brain. I think he may be mad."

Martala looked at me. We said nothing in response to this strange remark.

Chapter Seven

Several hours passed. I grew bored and wanted to explore the monastery but Martala forbade it, fearing that Nicodemus was testing us to see what we would do. After fidgeting with my dagger for a time, I spread a sheepskin on the floor and lay down on it.

A light knock on the door roused me from my doze. I stood quickly and drew my dagger. The women were lying on the bed. Martala got to her feet and nodded to me. Approaching the door with caution, I opened it a crack and saw that it was the same nun we had passed in the hallway earlier. Sheathing my weapon, I stood aside.

"I will escort you to the dining hall, Lady Pakali," she said in a meek voice, her head bowed.

My father's house has many servants. I have lived with them all my life. I would have recognized the signs of abuse even had the purple bruise on her cheek not been so prominent.

"What is your name, child?" Martala asked.

"I am Sister Ruth."

"Wait a moment in the corridor, Sister Ruth. We will join you shortly."

I closed the door. "Are we to leave our packs behind us?" I asked in a low voice. "They are likely to rob us."

"We can scarcely carry the packs on our backs into the dining hall," Martala said.

"They will not rob us," Anisah said. Her tone was confident.

"How do you know that?" I asked.

"The Abbot Nicodemus believes our gold and everything else we possess belongs to him. No one else in this place would dare to touch it."

"You are very perceptive," Martala said.

"I feel things sometimes, or sense things. Father says it is one of the gifts that descended to me from my mother."

"A queen of faerie."

"Yes, so Father says."

"Should I wear my sword and dagger?" I asked Martala.

"I think not. We wish to appear peaceful and trusting."

We left the bedchamber together. Sister Ruth escorted us to a small room where we could wash our hands and faces in a stone basin that was filled with cold water, and relieve ourselves in a privy.

As we continued on behind her, from somewhere else in the monastery a brass gong sounded three strikes. We came to an intersection of the corridors, and passed an enormous set of oaken doors that entirely filled one of its four branching ways. The scent of burning sulfur was strong.

"If I may inquire, Sister Ruth, what lies beyond these doors?"

The nun cast a frightened glance at me over her shoulder. "We must hurry, or we will be late for the seating."

The white-robed monks were standing behind the benches of two long tables that ran most of the length of the dining hall, which was a narrow chamber extending back into the mountain. At its far end a large fireplace had been carved into the rock. Painted portraits of saints decorated all its walls.

In front of the fireplace, which was not burning, eight nuns stood around a smaller table with bowed heads. They were separated by some distance from the tables of the monks.

Sister Ruth escorted us to the front of the hall where light flooded in through a row of large windows. At the end of one of the long tables were three vacant places. I noticed that the monks standing around them were older than their brothers further down the table. Seniority had its privileges, even in a house of the Christian god. The head of the table was occupied by an ornately carved wooden armchair with a high back.

Steam rose from large bowls and platters of food that had already been placed on the boards. My nose told me the platters of sliced meat most likely held roast pork. The soup in the silver tureens appeared to be vegetable. There were fresh fruits, platters of sliced brown bread, butter and cheese. Whatever else might be said about the monks of the Order of Ambrose, they were not starving. We took our standing places, and Sister Ruth withdrew to the far end of the hall to stand with the other nuns. There was complete silence.

Heavy footfalls sounded from an archway. The Abbot emerged and went to the head of the table. He stood behind the armchair and placed his great hands on its back, gripping its upper edge. One of the monks in the hall took up a standing place at his left elbow, I presume to serve him when the time came. It was probably a position of honor.

"Today our noon repast is blessed by the company of pilgrims who have traveled from far Alexandria, in Egypt, to be with us. Let us welcome them."

A murmur of welcome filled the hall. It sounded sincere enough to my ears, but it was mixed with a ripple of quiet laughter, which I found disturbing.

An older monk who stood near the side wall midway down the chamber silently approached what I perceived to be a kind of lectern, upon which rested a large book. The Abbot and the monks bowed their heads. Opening the book at a red ribbon that hung between its pages, the elder monk began to read in a high but clear voice in Greek.

"It is true, without falsehood, and free from all error that what is below is like to that which is above, and what is above is like to that which is below, for the miraculous

45

accomplishment of its single purpose. As all things are engendered from the seed of one, and so all things are born from one in their diversity. The sun is its father, the moon its mother, the wind carries it to term in its belly, its birthing is in the earth. The source of all perfection is here. Its power is manifest if it be reduced to its salts. Gently and with great care separate the salts from the spirit, the subtle from the gross. Ascend into the heavens and descend again to the earth. The matter is most potent when transfigured by flame, for it will vanquish any vapor and penetrate any solid. Thusly shall you accomplish all, and obscurity will fly from you. Hence I am Jesu, the Christ of the Trinity, having the three parts of holy wisdom. That which I had to say concerning the Working of the Son has been fulfilled. Amen."

Martala, who was standing on my right side, glanced at me with a raised eyebrow. I nodded to her. The text was not composed of verses from the Christian gospels. Its wording was somewhat different in Arabic, but I recognized it from my studies as Hermetic, and alchemical.

Without further ceremony, the Abbot sat in his chair and the monks at their benches. The silence was broken by the clatter of dining knives on pewter plates.

"Will you take some meat, Lady Pakali?" Nicodemus said to Martala. "It is quite fresh. The beast was only slaughtered this morning."

She nodded, and as if by magic a nun appeared at her side and placed a slice of the steaming pink meat on her plate.

I saw that the nuns did not remained seated at their own table, but got up and hurried to the tables of the monks each time one of the men gestured with his hand for assistance.

"Shall I help you with your plate?" I murmured to Anisah.

"Not the meat," she said. "Just some vegetable soup, and a slice of bread."

I filled her bowl before one of the nuns could rush over to do it for me, than took some meat and bread for myself. Martala chatted with the Abbot as she ate and seemed completely at her ease, as if she were accustomed to attending large feasts. The meat was good—better than I expected. I found myself taking a second slice. The mountain air had invigorated my appetite.

The Abbot kept asking Martala questions about Alexandria. I realized that he was testing her, attempting to find an error in her replies. She answered him without hesitation. It was soon evident that her knowledge of Alexandria was greater than his own, so he gave up the effort. Then he said something that chilled me. "You are such a great traveler, may I ask you what you think of the city of Damascus?"

"What of Damascus?" she said her voice unvarying.

"I have heard it said that may great wizards dwell there. It is said they even have their own street."

"The Lane of Scholars," she said. "I have heard of it, but have never walked upon it during my visits to the city."

"I thought perhaps there might be a master of alchemy there who could give you instruction."

"I believe the Lane does boast an alchemist or two, but as to their worth, I cannot say. None of them shares your reputation."

"What of necromancers?" he said with a smile, his lips and beard gleaming with grease. "I have been told that great necromancers dwell in the street."

A chillness gripped my chest. Under the table, Anisah's hand sought out mine. I squeezed her fingers but did not turn my head from my plate.

"As to that, I really have no information to impart," Martala said. "Necromancy has never been a study of interest to me."

"Of course not. All those rotting corpses. You are too fine a lady to be burdened by such horrors. A virtue of alchemy is that all its processes are cleansed by fire and thus purified."

"It is the sacred art of kings."

"Indeed. They do call it the royal way. Yet we who follow it are only humble pilgrims, like yourself."

"May I ask, have you come to a decision as to my status?"

He laughed, the sound rumbling in his great chest like distant thunder. "You must not press me, Lady Pakali. As I have told you, I will give you my answer tomorrow."

"Forgive my forwardness. It is only that I thirst for the wisdom of your art. Is it true that you can control the portals of Yog-Sothoth, summoning them and opening them at will?"

"You know a great deal more about our work than you indicated when we spoke earlier," he said, his pale blue eyes narrowing.

"It is wise to be discreet," she said.

"Very true. If you are accepted as my student, you will learn all the things you seek to know."

An elderly monk whose deeply lined face hung down like an empty sack motioned for assistance. A nun hurried to his side. I recognized Sister Ruth by the bruise on her cheek before I remembered her features. She lifted an earthenware pitcher from the table to fill the old man's cup. The handle snapped, and red wine poured over his plate and into his lap.

"You stupid slut, watch what you are doing," he roared, and struck her with his open hand on the face.

"I apologize, holy brother," she said in a meek voice.

"I don't want your apology; bring me a towel."

I found my hand reaching to my side where my sword should have hung. What I might have done had I been wearing it, I do not know, but my blood was up and my face flushed with anger. I half rose from the bench, and Martala laid her hand on my thigh, pressing me back onto the seat.

Chapter Eight

The meal continued as though no incident had occurred. When it was over, we were escorted to our room by an older, pinch-faced nun who did not offer her name or even speak. This time, when the door shut, I heard the bolt slide into place on its other side.

"The Abbot knows who we are," I said to Martala.

"We can't be sure of that. The mention of Damascus may have been nothing more than chance."

"And the remarks about the Lane of Scholars? And necromancers?"

"How could he possibly know who we are?"

This question left me silent. I could think of no way Nicodemus could have learned our true identity or our purpose—for if he knew one, it was not unreasonable to suspect he also knew the other.

"The women here are treated as slaves," Anisah said. "It is horrible."

"Mayhap you will see many horrible things before this quest is ended," Martala told her. "You have led a sheltered life, Anisah, but you are not in your father's house today, you are in the greater world, and it is filled with worse horrors than you can imagine."

"Be kind to the girl," I said. "She is not accustomed to such violence."

"I sorrow for the women," Anisah said.

"As do we," I told her gently. "But you will soon learn that there are many injustices in this world that we cannot solve. They must be endured."

Martala walked over to where our packs had been placed to examine them.

"The rug is gone," she said.

I hurried over and saw that she was correct. The carpet that had carried us to Soumela was nowhere to be found.

"Perhaps someone took it away to be cleaned," Anisah said.

I looked at Martala. Her eyes were like chips of ice. We both knew that our charade was at an end. Whether the Abbot knew our purpose or not, he had no intention of honoring his promises. No one would have stolen such a threadbare and dirty carpet unless they suspected its true nature. Again I wondered if our arrival had been observed from the monastery gallery, or from one of the windows.

"If he means to kill us, why hasn't he done so?" I asked Martala.

"I don't know. Perhaps he is waiting for something, or for someone."

I picked my sword and dagger up from the floor and belted them around my waist, vowing to myself not to remove them again until we were out of danger. They would be useless against more than half a hundred monks, but their weight comforted me.

Going to the door, I tried its latch. It rattled but the door did not open.

"We are trapped until Nicodemus decides to let us out."

"Not necessarily," Martala said.

She held a small dagger with a broad blade in her hand. I wondered where it had come from. I had not previously seen it in her pack or upon her person. She went to the door and slid the blade into the crack between the door and the doorjamb at the level of the latch. It was a very narrow crack—neither my sword nor my dagger would have fitted into it, but the Egyptian woman's little dagger had an uncommonly thin blade.

"We'll wait until the monks are sleeping, then explore this place."

"What if we find nothing that concerns the fate of Alhazred?"

"There has to be something here. Alhazred was interested in Soumela for a reason. If anyone knows what that reason was, it will be Nicodemus. We'll go to his bedchamber and persuade him to tell us."

"Persuade? You mean by torture?"

"Would he say anything otherwise?"

A sickness came into my stomach. Criminals were tortured for their crimes. That was to be expected. But I had never witnessed torture nor felt a desire to participate in such a barbarity, which was suited only to those of a low station in life.

The wait was long. A distant bell sounded the hours. At last Martala judged enough time had passed for the monks to have retired to their cells. She went to the door and busied herself with the latch. I saw Anisah shiver.

"Are you frightened?" I asked gently.

"Something is not right," she said, her teeth chattering even though there was no chill in the room.

"In what way?"

"I don't know. I feel the wrongness, but it has no shape that I can identify."

"We have put ourselves into a dangerous circumstance. It is no shame to be afraid."

"I do not fear for myself." She laid her hand on my arm. "I know you will defend us bravely with your sword."

"Got it," Martala said.

She opened the door as silently as the wrought iron latch would allow. We moved quietly into the lamp-lit corridor, which was empty.

"I want to know what's behind those great doors we passed," she said.

"There was a strong smell of sulfur," I said. "Sulfur is a prime component in the processes of alchemy."

"You divine my thoughts."

"No one walks the halls," Anisah said. "They are all asleep."

I glanced at Martala, who shrugged. There was no way to know how far we could trust the girl's intuition.

When we reached the massive oak doors, we found one of them ajar.

"This I do not like," Martala murmured. She extended her dagger before her and used her other hand to pull the heavy door wider. On the other side there was darkness.

As silent as three mice, we slid our bodies through the gap and into the shadows. The stench of burning sulfur was strong, and the air felt warm and moist. Somewhere far ahead a lamp burned, casting a dim red glow over the walls of the corridor. We moved along its length with small steps, keeping closely together. My hand rested on the hilt of my sword.

The corridor bent to the right. On the left was a closed door of no great size. Martala put her ear to its planks, then tried its latch. It opened. A wash of frigid air spilled out and flowed around us like invisible water. Glancing at me, she entered. I followed close behind. Inside was utter darkness. Listening, I heard no sound but that of our own movements. Sparks flew from a place a few steps before me. I realized that Martala was striking flint to ignite her tinderbox. Flames flickered on the tinder and brightened.

All around us hung slabs of meat from hooks in the ceiling. The meat had been quartered and skinned. Along the walls of the chamber were stacked huge blocks of ice that were wrapped in woven straw blankets.

"This must be the monastery larder," I murmured. My voice sounded unnaturally loud in my ears. "From here came the pork that was on the dining hall tables."

"Not pork," Anisah whispered close behind me. She pointed past my shoulder.

From one of the hooks hung upside down the body of a naked woman whose abdomen had been split open. Her organs had been removed, and her pale skin was covered in dried blood. Her dead eyes stared up at me. I recognized the bruise on her cheek.

"Discipline is severe at Soumela," Martala said.

My body would not obey me. I stumbled to the corner and vomited onto the stone floor next to a block of ice. For a time I remained doubled over, too dizzy to stand. I spat out the sour taste and wiped my mouth with my hand, then wiped my hand on my tunic. Straightening, I saw Martala watching me, her face expressionless.

"Are you done?" she asked.

I felt my cheeks flush with embarrassment and said nothing.

"You were wise to refuse the pork," Martala told the girl. "There is nothing here for us."

We followed her out and down the side branch of the corridor. The air became hotter as we advanced. At length we came to a long gallery with pillars running down either side. We slid through the door and advanced along the left wall, silent as shadows. A dozen men robed in black were gathered in the middle of the chamber, all of them armed with swords and daggers. On the floor painted in red was a complex occult pentacle that had the form of a double circle within which was delineated a star of eight points formed by two overlapping squares. Words were written in Hebrew script between the lines of the circle.

Not far from where the monks stood, a fire burned inside a kind of conical furnace made of bricks. The smoke was vented through a hole in the ceiling, but the air of the gallery was laden with the stench of sulfur. The fire flared up, and I glimpsed a large glass vessel within the furnace upon its glowing embers. Something black moved within the transparent shell.

Behind the row of pillars on the left side of the gallery were ranged enormous earthenware vessels and wooden crates. Along the wall stood shelves filled with jars, vials and bowls of different shapes and sizes. Some of them resembled jars I had glimpsed in the cellar of Alhazred's house in Damascus.

By crouching behind the crates we were able to draw near enough to hear what the monks were saying. I recognized the Abbot Nicodemus by his booming voice and bristling beard, although he now wore a black robe trimmed in red instead of the scarlet garment he had worn earlier. He was in animated discussion with another black-robed monk who was almost as tall as him, but not as fleshy through the belly. There was a familial resemblance between the two.

"I tell you, Brother Lucius, this carpet carried the woman and her servants here by some magic. With my own eyes I saw them appear at the base of a whirlwind that flashed lightning and sparkled with many colors."

He held under his arm the carpet roll stolen from our bedchamber.

"Let us see this magic carpet," the monk called Lucius said in a harsh voice.

Nicodemus untied it and spread it on the floor amid the other curious black-robed monks, who formed a circle around it. Lucius regarded it for a moment, then laughed.

"This worn-out old rug is not even fit for a dog to sleep on."

"I know what I saw," Nicodemus said.

He stood on the carpet and waited in expectation. When nothing happened, a ripple of suppressed laughter ran around the ring of monks.

"Carpet, carry me to the steps of the Hagia Sophia in Constantinople," the Abbot said in a commanding voice.

"Do you know how foolish you look, Brother?" Lucius said.

"That Egyptian woman must know some secret word to make it fly," Nicodemus murmured. He stomped his boot heel heavily on the carpet. "Carpet, heed me. I am your master now."

The hem of the carpet rippled and lifted, as though borne up on a breeze.

"Did you see that?" Nicodemus asked.

"I see nothing, Brother, only you, acting the fool, as usual."

Nicodemus cursed and stepped off the carpet. He kicked it aside.

"I'll torture that Egyptian bitch and learn its secret before we butcher her."

"We can't kill them until we communicate with our misshapen cousins on the Plateau of Leng. They may have other uses for them."

"To the Devil with those deformed monsters," Nicodemus said. "Yog-Sothoth favors us. We don't need them to intercede for us any longer."

"Need I remind you, Nicodemus, it was they who gave us advance warning that Alhazred's Egyptian bitch would try to come here? They have eyes and ears everywhere."

"As well they should," the Abbot said, and the two men laughed heartily.

I wondered what the jest might be, for I could think of no reason for laughter.

"Now that we can open the gates, we no longer need to do their bidding, Nicodemus said, returning to his theme. "They treat us like their thralls. I'm sick of smiling at their ugly faces."

The fire in the brick furnace flared up brightly, casting red light across the brutal features of the monk named Lucius. Anisah let out a stifled scream. All the monks turned in our direction.

Chapter Nine

"id you hear that?" Lucius said. "It sounded like a woman."

"Search the stores," Nicodemus ordered.

I looked back the way we had entered. We would surely be seen if we tried to escape. There was nothing to do but crouch lower and hope we were not discovered. Luck was not with us.

"Here, behind the amphorae," one monk cried out.

In moments they surrounded us, forcing us to move into the middle of the gallery.

I drew my sword and dagger, determined to protect the women at the cost of my own life. There was little doubt as to the outcome. The black-robed monks drew their own weapons as they advanced in a ring around us.

I stepped in front of Martala and saw with some surprise that she was not holding her dagger.

"Put down your weapons, Hassid," she said in a level tone. "There are too many of them."

I would have disobeyed her, but she placed her hand on my sword arm and forced it downward firmly.

The monks rushed forward and tore the weapons from me.

"I know this girl," Lucius said, excitement rising in his voice. He grabbed Anisah by the wrist and dragged her closer to the glow from the furnace. He laughed loud and long.

"Are you going to share the jest?" Nicodemus asked in irritation.

"This is the daughter of the necromancer Harkanos. She is the one I have been watching all these years, waiting for her to emerge from the protection of her father's house so that she could be abducted."

Anisah turned to me with a look of anguish.

"These are the monks who took me from my father's house when I was only a child," she said in a shaking voice. "The monks who killed me." She pointed at Lucius. "He was their leader."

"I am still their leader," he said, smiling through his black beard. "I see that your rebirth from your essential salts has given you a voice. Splendid. I will soon find good use for it."

"You have changed your spots," Martala said.

Nicodemus looked down at his robe and laughed. "Both white and black are the colors of our art, as you should know, if you have really studied it."

"How did you know I was coming here?" she demanded.

I was amazed at the firmness of her voice, which did not waver. As for myself, my heart was beating like a blacksmith's hammer, although I did my best not to show it.

"Did Alhazred think the sprites he sent to probe this monastery and steal our secrets would not be noticed?" Nicodemus said. "We too can send agents to spy on our enemies. They saw and heard all that he intended."

"Our brother alchemists, the Shenghuo on the Plateau of Leng, were even less amused by his attempts to spy on their work," Lucius said, chuckling at the memory.

"Was it you who sent the demon that killed Alhazred in the Damascus marketplace?"

"We would have used a more conventional assassin," Lucius said.

"So it was the ones you call Shenghuo."

"As to that, who can say? Alhazred had many enemies. I have heard that his death was quite spectacular. I only wish I had been there in Damascus to witness it."

"Why was Alhazred spying on you?" Martala asked.

They looked at each other and laughed. "Did he not tell you?" Nicodemus said. "That is too amusing. I don't think I will tell you, either."

"We need to have our little black man open the portal to Leng, so that we can inform the Shenghuo brothers that their guests have arrived," Nicodemus said.

"I don't like sending them the girl," Lucius said. "I don't want to risk losing her again."

"You can tell them that yourself when the gateway is opened," Nicodemus said with a smile. "But you won't, will you, Brother? Because that might make them angry."

"I am not their servant!" Lucius said in a voice that rang from the walls like the clash of steel. His dark eyes flashed with anger.

"Patience, Brother, patience," Nicodemus said soothingly. He put his hand on the other monk's shoulder. "Soon we will have obtained everything we need. Then we can dispense with them."

"The great secret doesn't belong in the paws of those deformed freaks," Lucius said. "It should be ours."

"All in good time, Lucius."

Nicodemus turned to a monk who stood near and murmured. The lesser brother gestured to another man. They took down a large iron set of tongs and advanced upon the furnace. Fitting the looped end into the fire, they lifted with some difficulty the glass vessel out and set it on a platform of brick. Sparks brightened and died on the blackened surface of the vessel, which was shaped like a giant egg with a wide mouth at its top. This opening was stopped with a plug of some glowing material.

"Release him," Nicodemus ordered.

The monks used a set of pinchers to peel back the lid from the vessel. I saw that it was inscribed with arcane symbols. They stepped back in haste, as though fearful.

Something stirred within its depths. A tiny hand and arm reached up through the opening, followed by another hand

and arm. The hands gripped the rim, and a head emerged. It was completely black, not black like the skin of a Negro, but with the blackness of soot. With its large ears and round shape it somewhat resembled the head of a monkey, but there was a malign intelligence in the bright eyes that darted from side to side as it examined its surroundings.

The creature grinned showing white, pointed teeth, then began to work his body out of the vessel, the opening of which was as tight around it as bark around a tree. After much labor he stood swaying on the platform on his bowed legs, completely naked. His oversized male member was prominently erect. In height he was no more than a cubit.

"Homunculus," Martala said softly.

"You know something of the art after all," Nicodemus said. "This little man was created to serve us."

"But not created by you," Anisah said.

The Abbot looked at her in mild surprise. "You are very perceptive. No, not by us. He was a gift from our Shenghuo friends on the Plateau of Leng."

The homunculus climbed off the brick platform to the floor and stood staring insolently at Nicodemus with his bright little eyes, which reminded me of black olives set inside slices of boiled egg.

"Little man, I have a question," Nicodemus said. He pointed at the carpet on the floor. "Does this carpet fly?"

The homunculus chittered in laughter and nodded up and down vigorously.

"It is the flying carpet that was used by Solomon the Great," he said in a voice that was almost childlike.

"You lie. The carpet of Solomon was enormous, and richly colored."

"Are you so sure?" The homunculus cocked his grotesque head to one side.

"So say all the tales."

"That may be, but how many tellers of those tales ever saw it?"

The Abbot frowned in thought. "If this truly is the flying carpet of Solomon, it is a pearl beyond price," he said to Lucius.

"I care nothing about carpets," Lucius said with a dismissive gesture. "I care only about the great secret of the art." He pointed at the homunculus. "Open the gate to Leng, monster."

The homunculus bowed low, but I detected contempt in the gesture. He crossed the floor to the red pentacle and began to dance inside it, his tiny voice reciting words in an uncouth, guttural language. Several times during this incantation he repeated a name familiar to me—Yog-Sothoth.

"You know the secret to command Solomon's carpet," Nicodemus said to Martala.

"I do."

"Reveal it to me and I may let you live after the Shenghuo are done with you."

Martala hesitated.

"I can torture it out of you," the Abbot said. "Our Order has refined torture to an exquisite degree. Pain tenderizes our meat, you see, and infuses it with a life-giving essence that prolongs our years. How old would you say I am?"

"I don't know."

"I am one hundred and forty-seven. My brother Lucius is one hundred and thirty-nine." He motioned for a monk to approach. It was the same young monk who had admitted us to the monastery. "How old are you, Brother Cyril?"

"Fifty-seven years," the monk said.

"Now do you see the power of our art? Speak, woman. Or perhaps you would prefer that I torture the girl?"

Martala hesitated, or pretended to hesitate.

"Very well, I'll tell you. The carpet is hungry. It must have blood."

The faded-blue eyes of the Abbot widened with excitement. He looked at me, and took a step toward me.

"Our Shenghuo brothers were very specific," Lucius murmured. "All the spies are to be sent to them alive."

Nicodemus hesitated, glared hatred at me, then turned and in a single motion dragged one of the monks who stood near him over the carpet and slashed the man's throat with his dagger. Blood poured from the wound onto the threadbare carpet. What had happened with the wine was repeated with the blood. It sank into the nap and disappeared without leaving a stain. The Abbot cast the corpse aside as easily as if it were a straw doll.

"Butcher this and hang it in the larder," he said. Two monks hastened to fulfill his instruction.

Above the pentacle, the air began to glow and swirl. A vertical oval formed that was six or seven cubits in height. It floated just above the floor, its rim flickering with blue fire, but its center was a kind of dark purple that seemed to be continuously falling into itself. The Abbot seemed unaware of the portal, so intense was his concentration on the carpet.

"Tell me what to do," he said to Martala.

"Step onto the carpet."

He did so.

The carpet rippled strongly, causing him to rise from the floor in spite of his great bulk. He laughed with delight.

"Now what?"

"Now you speak its name, and tell it where to carry you."

"Its name, tell me its name."

Lucius stood some distance away with an expression of exasperation. "We have not time for this foolishness, Brother."

"Tell me the name!" Nicodemus roared.

"The name is Ala-aljahim," Martala said.

"Ala-aljahim, carry me to the steps of the Hagia Sophia in Constantinople."

The carpet reared up on one side, almost throwing him off. He stamped down hard with his boot and ground the edge of its heel into the fabric.

"Obey me, Ala-aljahim, or I will have you slashed to threads."

Lucius stared at Martala. "What trickery is this?"

The carpet tilted, throwing the Abbot from his feet. Before he could get up, it rolled around his body. It seemed to stretch to cover him, so that in some remarkable manner every part of his great bulk was concealed within it. Undulations rippled down its length. Nicodemus let out a muffled roar that turned into a scream.

"I am here, Brother," Lucius said, rushing to the carpet, which bore some resemblance to a snake with a rat in its belly. He turned his head. "Help me, you fools."

The other monks hurried to his aid. They gripped the edges of the carpet. It flopped across the floor like a fish taken out of water, but they were not strong enough to open it. The screams continued to come forth.

I felt Martala's right hand in mine, and saw that she held Anisah's arm with her left.

"Quickly, with me."

She pulled us toward the shining oval gateway. The homunculus was watching the antics of the monks with evident delight. He let out a squawk when he saw us approach and tried to scurry out of the way, but my boot caught him, and the four of us tumbled through the portal together.

Chapter Ten

Something hard and cold pressed against my face. I pushed away with my hands and spat out pieces of grass that had found their way into my mouth. There was grass all around, tall shoots of broad-bladed grass. It hemmed me in on all sides as if trying to hold me prisoner. I looked about and saw nothing but grass. The breeze blew through it, and it rustled like a hissing serpent. It was green but turning brown in places, as grass will at the beginning of a dry season.

I had never seen so much grass. Its waving blades towered above me, swaying across the face of the sun, hiding most of the cold blue sky. Where the sun did touch my face, it held little warmth. The breeze chilled me, so much so that I shivered. I suddenly remembered the portal, and realized I was sitting on the Plateau of Leng, about which so many horrible things were hinted at in ancient and forbidden texts. Always before I had assumed it to be no more than a fable, yet here I was. This thought terrified me.

I leapt up, and discovered that the grass grew only as high as my breast. Not far away Martala was helping Anisah to her feet. She brushed bits of straw from the back of the girl, who looked at me with a bewildered expression.

"The little man," I said. "Where is the little man?"

"Gone," Martala said.

"Are we on Leng?" Anisah asked.

Martala stopped what she was doing with her hands and looked out across the sea of grass that rippled in waves where it was touched by the wind. It extended unbroken to the horizon in all directions. There were no mountains, no trees, no roads, no lakes, no traces of human occupation, only grass. She tilted her head. Her nostrils flared as she smelled the air, and I unconsciously imitated her. It was a strange scent, a mingling of soil, dust and dung overlaid by the smell of dry grass.

"Yes, this is the Plateau of Leng."

Her voice held a note of ominous foreboding. Or perhaps I only imagined it due to my own mounting apprehension. The portal was gone. It had taken everything I had ever known with it. I had no sword, no dagger. Our packs with all our food, water, and other supplies were presumably still in the Soumela Monastery, along with Solomon's carpet, if indeed the little black man had spoken the truth and it was the fabled flying carpet of King Solomon. I remembered that it had eaten Nicodemus. This offered some fleeting satisfaction. My thoughts were slow, as if my head were filled with smoke, but my awareness was beginning to clear.

"What are we going to do?" I asked.

Martala frowned at me. I realized my voice held a rising note of panic and forced it lower, speaking more slowly.

"We do not have any food or water. I've lost my sword and dagger, so I cannot defend you or even myself if we are attacked. We can't stay here, but we don't know where to go. And where is the homunculus? I remember kicking him through the portal."

"Calm yourself, Hassid. I have my dagger. I have my tinder box for making fires. All of us wear strong leather boots. Our situation could be much worse, I assure you."

Even as she spoke these words, a distant howl sounded on the air. It was drawn out like the howl of a wolf, but less musical. It was followed by a kind of coughing that could only come from the throat of a large beast.

"We should move," Martala said.

"But which way?"

She squinted at the sun. It was high in the sky. When we jumped through the portal it had been the middle of the night, but now it was noon. This made no sense, yet it was so.

"Salaymorlaynah said the monastery of the Shenghuo Sect lies in the north. If we walk with the sun at our backs we will be walking north."

"Yes, for a time at least, but what will we do after night falls, or when it becomes cloudy, or there is a mist?"

"Do you really expect me to have answers to those questions?"

I thought for a moment. "No, I suppose not."

"Then why ask them?"

We began to press our way between the waving blades of grass, which hid from out of sight the lower parts of our bodies, so that it almost seemed that we were floating. From time to time we heard a distant howl carried on the wind. Some beast was hunting its food. Thus far it had not been successful.

"This is the right direction," Anisah said after we had walked for a time.

"How can you be sure?" I asked.

"I just feel its rightness. I know it."

This was not a statement with which I could argue even had I felt the inclination to do so. I hoped the girl's intuition would not fail us.

We walked on through the long afternoon as the cold sun declined in the west. The grass was stiff and sharp—almost sharp enough to cut me when I brushed it aside with my hands. From it arose a kind of biting gnat that flew in clouds around our heads when disturbed. Its bites felt like the touch of red-hot needles on the skin. The women had head coverings, but I did not.

At length we came upon a shallow gully through which flowed a sluggish stream of water. It was so well hidden by the grass, we almost stepped into it.

"Drink deep," Martala said. "There is no way to know when we shall see water again."

I lay on my belly and cupped the water into my mouth with both hands. It had a slight coppery taste but was not foul. Anisah imitated my posture, but Martala knelt on one knee and lifted the water to her lips with only one hand. She stood and gazed across the plain.

"Something is coming," she said.

I leapt to my feet, my hand instinctively going to my left hip where my sword should have hung. From some distance away I heard the crackle and hiss of grass being thrust aside. It drew nearer. Martala crouched, and I saw the dagger in her hand gleam red as its blade caught and reflected the late afternoon sunlight. I pushed Anisah behind me and clenched my fists.

Almost at our feet, the little black man burst forth from the concealment of the grass at a run. He did not see the stream in time to stop and dashed into it, then fell on his face. He beat the water with his tiny arms, trying to get to his feet.

"Back up," Martala said harshly.

I stepped away from the wall of grass, pushing the girl along with me. From the grass emerged the head and shoulders of the most massive hound I have ever seen. It was almost as tall as I am. Its head was huge and blunt, like the head of a mastiff, but its ears stood upright. Short, black fur bristled on its shoulders and forelegs, one of which was bleeding. It shifted its weight and I saw that it favored the injured leg.

The beast eyed the three of us in turn. Its lips curled away from its teeth, and a deep rumble issued from its broad chest. I was dimly aware of the thrashings of the homunculus behind me. He still had not found his way out of the water.

"Kill it, kill it," the little man screamed and sputtered in his childlike voice.

"I have a better idea," I said. "We'll feed you to it, and then it will leave us alone."

"No, don't say that. I will help you. I know the way to the house of the Shenghuo Sect. Save my life and I will serve you."

The shrieks of the little creature might have been amusing under other circumstances. The great hound's tense muscles quivered and it took a half step forward. Martala did the same and showed the animal her dagger. I forced myself to stand my ground. There was no sense in running from such a beast. Even wounded and limping, it would easily catch us. I risked a glance back. The little man had managed to climb onto the far bank of the stream, where he stood shaking with terror.

The demon hound snapped its teeth, and white foam flew from its lips. It advanced another half step. Martala hesitated then moved to the side.

"Back away, Hassid," she said in a low voice.

I backed away from the beast on its opposite side, one hand grasping the arm of Anisah so that I would know where she was without turning my head.

The hound advanced cautiously. It eyed the homunculus with its glaring eyes, and the little man fell over backwards and sat in the mud, pumping his heels in a vain attempt to push himself backwards. The beast lowered its head and lapped the water of the stream. It drank for what seemed a long time, then straightened. With another deep growl at the homunculus, it crouched on its haunches and sprang forward, sailing through the air over the tops of the grass on the far bank. The sounds of its progress through the grass diminished to silence.

"I don't think it likes you," I said.

The ugly little monkey face glared at me with hatred. He pushed himself up to his feet. I saw that his penis was still erect, as it had been in the monastery, and decided that must be its constant state.

Martala crossed the stream and held her dagger close to the creature's face.

"Did you mean what you said?"

"My word is true. I will serve you," he said.

"Why was the beast so eager to get at you?"

He shrugged his bony shoulders and tilted his head to the side. "I may have injured its leg with a sharp flint. I thought it was hunting me."

"If it wasn't hunting you then, it's hunting you now," I said.

The homunculus pressed his tiny hands to his chest. His abject terror was obvious.

"Keep me safe, and I will lead you to the house of the Shenghuo. That is your wish, is it not?"

"My wish is to recover the remains of Abdul Alhazred, a necromancer of Damascus," Martala said.

He cackled in a way I did not like.

"Do you know where they lie?" she asked.

"I have heard things spoken about this necromancer."

"What was spoken?"

"That he has been dealt with as the Shenghuo were ordered to deal with him."

"Ordered? Who gave this order?"

"That I don't know," the little man said. "The Shenghuo do not take me into their confidence."

"His remains, are they within the house of the Shenghuo?"

"Perhaps, or perhaps not. You must look for yourself."

A question occurred to me. "Why did you place your portal so far away from their dwelling place?"

He glared up at me with contempt. "You kicked me through the gate before I could fix its location. You are lucky we did not emerge at the bottom of the sea or among the stars."

"Enough talk. Lead us," Martala said.

We followed the homunculus until twilight. In spite of his diminutive stature he moved with surprising quickness.

When darkness began to close in, the three of us beat down the grass in a large circle while the little man watched. There was nothing to burn, but Martala used her dagger to dig up sections of the thick sod until we had a fire pit. She applied the flaming cotton in her tinder box to the dry grass, and the sods began to smolder and glow redly.

"We must be careful with the fire," she said as she tended it with her dagger.

I looked all around at the grassland, gray in the twilight, and found myself in full agreement. A fire could be fatal, if a wind blew up.

The burning sod gave a surprising amount of warmth. We three sat around it, but the homunculus climbed directly into its center and curled his naked body like a salamander. In minutes he appeared to fall asleep.

I looked up past the rising column of white smoke. The stars were impossibly bright and seemed near enough to pluck from the black velvet of the firmament. Around us we heard howls that must have come from the throats of great hounds as they hunted their prey, but they were distant. I wonder if the wounded beast was out there in the darkness, watching us through the grass.

"Perhaps you should give me your dagger," I said to Martala, who was busy braiding grass into a kind of rope.

She frowned. "Why would I do that?"

"I am the only man here. It is my duty to protect you and Anisah, but I have no weapon. I am stronger than you. . . ."

"I doubt that."

"I am stronger than you and should carry the knife, since there is only one."

"I'm not giving you my dagger, so put that notion out of your head."

I fell into a brooding silence. I was not accustomed to being spoken to in that way by a woman. Even my own mother showed me more respect.

I watched her take one of the stones she had dug out of the fire pit and weave a kind of grass cage around it. This she fastened to the end of her length of grass rope. She stood with it and whirled the stone around her head on the end of the rope, then dashed it to the ground. It left a dent in the sod.

"This will not stand much use, but it is the only weapon I could make for you. Try the weight of it."

I stood and accepted the rope, then imitated her and spun the stone around my head. Catching the stone in my left hand, I studied it in amazement. She had crafted a kind of war-mace from nothing but grass and a piece of rock.

"I doubt it would do much good against that hell-hound, but it might slow the beast down enough for me to slit its throat," she said, and yawned. "Get some sleep, Hassid. You will need it."

Lying down beside Anisah, who was already asleep with her back to the fire, she fell silent. I spun the stone around my head several more times to become familiar with its weight, should I need to use it in our defense. I felt eyes upon me. The homunculus was sitting on the glowing blocks of sod with his bowed legs crossed, watching me with an expression of contempt. I repressed the impulse to send the stone dashing down on his misshapen head.

"Do you have a name?" I asked him in a low voice so as not to wake the women.

"Perhaps."

"Am I to be permitted to know what it is?"

"No."

"I could beat it out of you."

"That would be a breach of our compact. I would steal away and leave you and these women to wander lost upon the plain until the hounds caught your scent. They would make short work of you."

With this cheerful picture in my mind, I lay down near the fire and went to sleep.

Chapter Eleven

In the early morning I used the stone mace to kill a rabbit that wandered incautiously to the edge of our circle. We made breakfast with its meager flesh, roasted over a sod fire in a woven basket of grass. I decided it was the best meat I had ever tasted, but I longed for a drink of water, even so little as a single swallow.

"Don't you ever get thirsty?" I asked the little man, who was stretching himself out on the embers of the fire.

"Not for water."

"How much farther is it to the house of the Shenghuo?" Martala asked.

He tilted up his face and sniffed the breeze. "Nine days. Or maybe eleven. But certainly no more than thirteen."

"You will lead us to the nearest streams or ponds along the way, so that we can get water."

"There are many streams crossing the plain between here and the house of the Shenghuo. You will not die from thirst." The implication in his words was obvious.

The chill of the breeze became a kind of blessing as we labored to press through the midge-infested grassland. The little man seemed unimpeded. He passed between the grass the way a flea crawls through cat fur, with a kind of sidling, twisting motion of his body. Martala was tireless. She followed closely on the heels of the homunculus. Anisah was also strangely unaffected by the exertion of fighting her way through the grass. It almost appeared to part for her of its own accord. I wondered if it was her faerie blood that caused this magic, then decided that I was probably just imagining it due to the unnatural grace of her movements.

Of all the party I suffered the most. The effort of ceaselessly pushing against the grass exhausted me and made me sweat. Midges and other blood-sucking insects found the taste delicious. My legs trembled with fatigue. I wanted to stop and raise my fist to the heavens to curse the Plateau of Leng, but would not give the Egyptian woman the satisfaction of seeing me display such weakness. Although she had never spoken of it, I knew she expected the ordeal of the quest to break my spirit. I had no intention of showing her how close that was to happening.

That afternoon I managed to kill two rabbits with my mace. Martala found a large turtle in the water hole where we stopped to make camp at twilight. The meat roasting over our sod fire sent a savory smoke into the air. Perhaps that is what attracted the hound, or it may be that it had never ceased to follow us. I saw it lurking just beyond the edge of our camp circle. It caught my gaze and licked its lips.

"The beast is hungry," Anisah said to me. I realized she was watching it.

"We're all hungry."

"You should feed it," she said. "Its leg is injured. It can't hunt its own food."

"Don't be foolish. We barely have enough meat for ourselves."

"Listen to the girl," Martala said from the other side of the fire. "Give it some meat."

Shaking my head, I went to the fire and pulled off a leg from one of the rabbits, then tossed it into the wall of grass. The great beast snapped it up. I heard its bones crunch and grind between the hound's teeth. The animal looked at me for a moment, then turned and was gone with only a rustle to mark its passage.

"What are you muttering about?" Martala demanded.

"The foolish compassion of women," I said. "We can't afford to be kind to every stray dog. Such weakness will get us all killed."

"Perhaps you have a point," she said, but she did not sound convinced.

After that, the hound came to our campfire each evening. Against my better judgment, I was persuaded by Anisah to toss it a small portion of our meat, which we seldom failed to find due to the abundance of small game on the grassland. In spite of the quickness of these animals, they did not try to run from us, perhaps because they had never before been hunted by men. In addition to rabbits and turtles, there was a kind of wild chicken that could not fly, and so could be killed with thrown stones.

It was on the evening of the tenth day that the hunting pack found us, then closed in around our circle as we sat before our meager fire. The sun had already set and the sky had turned from blue to gray. There was no breeze to stir the grass, so we clearly heard them pushing through the long blades toward us on every side. They did not howl, but they panted in the expectation of tasting our blood.

"Stand with your backs to the fire," Martala said. "All beasts fear the flames."

The three of us stood back-to-back around the fire, while the homunculus cowered on its embers. The thought came to me that if only we could do the same, we might be safe, but I did not really believe it. Why would such hell-beasts fear fire?

We saw their eyes first, reflecting the firelight through the curtain of grass that stood at the edge of the clearing we had made. At least a dozen pairs of red sparks gleamed from the shadows. They were so close, I could hear them breathing.

I tightened my fingers on the length of grass rope and cradled the stone of my crude mace in my left hand. Anisah bent and picked up two smaller stones that had been dug from the sod while making the fire pit. The heat from the flames felt uncomfortably warm on my legs and back, but I did not dare step forward.

They pressed their snarling snouts through the grass into the red glow from the fire. Their growls rumbled like distant thunder.

I could not take my eyes off their forepaws, which were armed with curved black nails as long as my little finger. One hound who must have been their leader, for it was larger than the others, emerged into the clearing and crouched down on its hind legs, preparing to spring upon me. Its face was twisted with killing fury.

Something flashed past me. I saw that it was the hound that had followed us and begged from our campfire. It confronted the beast that had crept out of the grass and let out a kind of roar. The other members of the pack ceased to move forward and stood motionless, watching this confrontation, which I sensed was motivated by more than just a desire of the solitary animal to preserve its food source. The two beasts seemed to recognize each other. The foreleg of the begging hound had begun to heal, and was marked only by a scab of dried blood where the flint of the homunculus had wounded it.

Without warning, both beasts leapt forward and locked in battle. Their demonic howls, growling, and the snapping of their jaws was deafening. The other hounds began to howl in sympathy, but none of them interfered with the fight, which I realized must be for supremacy of the pack.

The wounded hound was slightly larger than the other, but it still limped and favored its foreleg. The other animal saw this weakness and fastened its teeth in the scab of the wound. The injured animal let out a shrill scream of agony. It sought to bite the other hound on the back of the neck, but its neck was protected by a ridge of bristling fur. The animals rolled on the ground and into the fire, which caused the homunculus to leap out and dance away with a squawk. We all backed away from their ferocious killing fury and watched in awe.

The burning sods set the fur of the pack leader on fire. It howled and twisted out from under its foe. I thought it would run into the grass, but it turned at the edge of the clearing and stood its ground. Once more the two animals leapt toward each other. There was nothing wrong with the wounded hound's hind legs, and it was clearly the stronger of the two. It knocked the other animal backward and locked its enormous jaws on the other beast's throat. Smoke still arose from where the fire had singed its fur. The beast on its back fought for its life, writhing and twisting its entire body in an effort to throw off the death grip of its foe, but soon its movements began to weaken. The jaws at its throat had cut off its breath. It suffocated to death over what seemed an agonizing span of time. At last its convulsions ceased and it lay still.

The victor stood up and cast its gaze at the members of the pack. They slowly advanced with their heads bowed, making small whining sounds in their throats. They licked the face and neck of the wounded hound in recognition of its leadership.

"Now we are dead," I murmured to the others.

Several of the hounds began to creep toward us, but their new leader barked and snapped its teeth at them, causing them to back away with fawning postures. It approached Anisah, who did not cower back from its blood-soaked jaws. She stared into its eyes in silent communion. The animal went back to the corpse of its rival and nudged it with its nose, then looked at Martala.

"It wants you to cut off a piece of meat from the dead hound," Anisah said.

Martala looked at me with her eyebrows raised. I shrugged. We had no chance should the hounds decide to turn on us. We were forced to put our trust in the intuition of the girl.

Martala approached the dead animal cautiously with her dagger before her and knelt beside it. With quick efficient strokes of the blade, she cut off a part of the beast's muscular hindquarters and pulled it loose, then backed away with it in her arms. The hound regarded her for a moment. Then it looked from one member of the pack to another, and back at the dead animal. As if by some silent agreement, three hounds came forward and began to drag the corpse from the clearing and into the grass. In moments they vanished from sight, but the sound of their progress could be heard for some time. The victorious leader stared into Anisah's eyes. She said nothing, but it seemed to understand her. It nodded its great head. Turning, it leapt into the grass, and the other watchful hounds followed it.

I marvelled at the intelligence of these uncanny beasts, which must far exceed that of any dog or wolf.

"It almost looked as though it were talking to you," I said to Anisah.

"So it was, but not with words."

"Forgive me for ever doubting the wisdom of allowing you to accompany us," Martala told her. "If not for you telling us to feed that creature, the pack would have torn us apart."

"We need not worry about the hounds for the rest of our journey," Anisah said. "We have been given safe passage across the plateau."

"How much farther until we reach the house of the Shenghuo?" I asked the little man, who was still trembling with terror. He blinked at me and sniffed the air.

"Another day. We are close."

Chapter Twelve

In the morning we continued to push through the seemingly endless grass, but as the sun reached its zenith the prospect changed. We found ourselves in a grove of evergreen trees. We passed between their needled boughs and emerged on the bank of a broad river. On the other side, some distance removed from the river where the ground was higher, stood a massive structure of black stone. From the middle of its roof rose a tower with four sides. We stopped to study the building. I could not see any windows, but there was a small doorway.

"Is that the house of the Shenghuo Sect?" Martala asked the little man.

"As you see, I have been true to my word," he said. "Now I am released from my bond with you."

"Not yet. There is still the river. How are we to cross it?"

The homunculus made no reply.

"Is there a ferry?"

His laughter was annoyingly shrill. "Who for? The hounds?"

Martala turned to me. "Can you swim?"

"That is not one of my skills," I admitted.

"What about you, Anisah?"

The girl studied the expanse of placid water, which flowed so slowly its surface was like a mirror. "I don't know. I've never tried."

"I don't suppose you can swim, either?" Martala said to the little black man, exasperation in her tone.

"I hate water."

"I am the only one who can swim. But if I cross the river I leave all of you behind. We must do it another way."

Along the river bank grew green reeds. Martala had us break them off at their bases and pile them up. She proceeded to bind them together into bundles using braided grass as twine. As sunset drew near, we found ourselves with a raft. Together we managed to drag and push it halfway into the water. To my surprise, it floated.

"We have no paddles and no sail," Martala said. "Anisah will lie with me on the left side, and Hassid will lie on the right. We will use our hands like paddles to push us through the water. It's fortunate the current is so slow."

"What of me?" the little man shrilled.

"Sit in the center and don't move around."

The women positioned themselves on the left side of the elongated vessel and the homunculus climbed to its center and lay flat, clutching its reeds. I pushed hard and managed to slide it over the black mud into the river, then climbed onto it. The raft tipped and rolled, very nearly throwing the women into the water. The weight of my body was almost enough to balance theirs, although it dipped down on its left side.

"This is not a stable boat," I murmured.

"It need only float for one crossing," Martala said between her teeth.

I managed by slow degrees to shift myself so that my right arm hung over the right side, and dipped my hand into the water, which was as cold as winter snow on the mountain.

"Don't fight the water," Martala instructed. "Paddle gently with your hands held flat. If we start spinning around we won't get anywhere."

By slow degrees we crept across the river.

Something brushed the back of my hand. With a stifled cry I snatched it out of the water. A shadow slid under the raft, lazy and undulating.

"Pull your hands out. There's something under us."

The women stopped paddling.

"What did you see?"

"I didn't see, I felt. Look, there it is."

A black shape rose high enough that its back broke the water. It was elongated and as thick around as my waist, but whether a long fish or a serpent I could not determine, for most of it stayed below the shining, rippled surface, which reflected the blue of the sky.

"If this were the Nile, it would be a crocodile," Martala said.

"Suppose it is still a flesh-eater?" I said.

"We could toss it the homunculus. That would give us time to paddle away from it."

The little man let out a loud squawk.

"You are very easy to make jest of," the Egyptian woman told him.

The homunculus began to curse her in some strange tongue. We all ignored him.

"What do you sense about this monster, Anisah?" I asked.

The girl did not speak for a time then said, "I sense slow, lazy thoughts. There is no lust for blood. I do not think it will harm us."

"In any case, we have no alternative," Martala said. "Paddle, Hassid, but do it gently so as not to stir the water."

In this way we continued across the river, nor did we catch another glimpse of the serpentine creature.

Our raft touched the reeds on its far bank. I climbed off the unstable craft nervously, looking all around, but saw no shadows beneath the surface. The water came up to my waist and my boots sank into the mud. With difficulty I clambered up the muddy bank and onto the dry ground. I saw the others had done the same.

The little man was able to jump from the front end of the raft to the reeds without getting wet, which pleased him to judge by the grin on his face as he surveyed the mud that covered our legs and boots.

We pulled the raft onto the bank as far as we were able and set about emptying our boots and wiping our trousers clean with handfuls of wadded grass. I tied my makeshift mace around my waist. Together we set off for the stone house, the little man leading us.

Chapter Thirteen

nly as we approached the black house of the Shenghuo did I begin to realize how enormous it was. The slabs of stone that formed its sides dwarfed any cut stones I had ever seen. I wondered where they had been quarried, and how they could possibly have been transported to this remote place. They must have come from hundreds or even thousands of miles away, for there was nothing like them on the part of the Plateau we had crossed.

The roof surrounding the central tower was made of flat black slabs, the edges of which projected over the walls. The four sides of the high trapezoidal tower narrowed toward the top. Each side appeared to be a single massive monolith. All the stones were cleanly cut and polished, so that they gleamed redly where the rays of the setting sun reflected from them.

The sun hung low in the west, almost touching the grass. It made me imagine a great eye filled with blood that watched our progress across this tableland as if we were insects crawling on a carpet. The massive walls of the black stone house that towered over our heads as we drew nearer reinforced this impression.

"If we enter freely, will we be taken prisoner by the monks? Will they kill us?" Martala asked the homunculus.

"Who can say? They do not share their confidences with

me. I am a thing to be created or destroyed, as it suits their whim."

There was bitterness in his childlike voice.

"Why do you continue to serve them?" I asked.

"I was made to serve. I have no other purpose. I can do nothing else."

"You could defy them," Martala said.

The little man made no response. As we drew near the door, which was constructed of age-blackened timbers held together with ornate straps of hammered iron, it opened silently. We stopped and regarded the shadows that lay inside.

"Follow me," the little man said.

The entrance hall was illuminated by oil lamps in brackets on its walls. The door closed behind us with a dull boom, moved by some unseen mechanism. I wondered if we were being watched. At the end of the corridor there was a kind of antechamber, brightly lit by many spherical lamps. Tapestries hung on the walls, and a large Persian carpet covered the center of the tiled floor.

A man in a yellow silk robe wearing a small black silk hat on his shaven head stood in the middle of the carpet, his hands concealed inside the wide sleeves of his robe in front of his waist. Embroidered on the robe in green and gold was a serpentine dragon that undulated around his body. He bowed and regarded us with a slight smile. There was a foreign cast to his features. I recognized him as a member of the race that inhabits the land of Chin, far to the east of Persia. In the course of handling some of my father's trade dealings in Damascus I had encountered members of his race several times. My experience was that they were invariably polite, but revealed little of what they were thinking.

"Welcome to the house of the Shenghuo Brotherhood." he said in Greek.

The little man trotted forward on his short legs and bowed his ungainly head. "Have I fulfilled my task, Master?"

The monk, if such he may be called, looked at us. "You

84

have brought the companions of Abdul Alhazred to us. You have fulfilled your task."

"Thank you, Master." He started toward one of the archways that led from the antechamber.

"Where are you going?" Martala demanded.

"I have work to do and places to be," he said without turning his head. "I brought you here, as promised. My compact with you has been fulfilled."

"Why have we been brought here?" Martala asked the yellow-robed monk.

"I was under the impression that you came of your own accord."

"So I once thought, but now I am thinking we would have ended up here no matter what our intention might have been."

"How perceptive of you. You must be Martala, Alhazred's companion."

"How do you know my name?"

"We know the names of each of you. This one is Anisah, daughter of the mage Harkanos, and this other is Hassid, son of Khaled ibn Umar, a wealthy trader of Damascus."

"If you know so much about us, why did you command the monks of the Soumela Monastery to send us here?"

"Our Enlightened Master wishes to grant you an audience."

"Why?"

"Of that he has not informed me."

"I hope you're not planning on eating us." My words were brash and uncouth, but they escaped my lips before I could stop them.

His smile widened to an almost imperceptible degree. "We are not so barbarous as our Christian associates. The members of our sect consume only plants for our sustenance."

I tried not to let it show on my face how much relief his words gave me. The image of the dead nun, gutted and strung upside down in the Soumela Monastery larder, still came to me when I closed my eyes. It turned my stomach.

As this thought passed through my mind, Sasha's human face seemed to materialize in the air before me.

If you wish, I can remove this image from your memory so that you will no longer be troubled by it, she said in my head.

That will not be necessary, I thought to her clearly, echoing the words in my mind. *But thank you for the offer.*

This exchange passed unnoticed by the women, but the monk eyed me with interest. "You are a most unusual party of travelers," he said. "If you will follow me, I will show you where you may wash yourselves and put on clean robes."

"We prefer to keep our own clothing," Martala said.

His dark eyes widened with faint horror. "As you wish. But you must allow us to clean them. Were we to present you to the Master in this state, it would shame us. We cannot allow it."

"Then show us where we can cleanse ourselves." She looked at me. "None of us will say no to a hot bath."

We followed him through an arch and along a corridor. Like the first, it was windowless and lit by burning lamps on the walls.

"I wonder why Brother Lucius called these monks deformed freaks?" I murmured to Martala, who walked beside me. "This one looks normal enough."

"Be alert against deceptions. I trust this smiling alchemist no more than I trusted the Abbot Nicodemus."

"He is hiding something," Anisah whispered behind us. "But I cannot sense what it may be."

We passed from the corridor into a long scriptorium filled with writing tables, where young monks in yellow robes sat copying scrolls. As I cast my gaze across their bent backs, my feet stumbled and I came to a standstill. The women stopped with me. We stared at the monks.

Several were missing their ears, or their noses. The lips of three were sewn closed apart from a small pipe that extended through a gap. Two monks were missing their feet. One held his pen in his left hand as he worked, for the right sleeve of his robe hung empty.

Our guide paused and turned. "Why have you stopped?" he asked mildly.

I pointed at the scribes. "What happened to them?"

"Nothing at all." Enlightenment dawned on his face. "Ah, I perceive your meaning." He walked back toward us. "Our sect believes that the senses of the body are conduits of evil that poison our souls and render them unfit for the heaven ordained to us in prophecy. In defiance of this source of corruption, each brother voluntarily relinquishes a bodily sense upon joining our Brotherhood. Those of extreme devotion may sacrifice two senses."

"What is wrong with his mouth?" I pointed to the monk whose lips had been sewn shut.

"That is Brother Lee, who has renounced the sense of taste, and has had his tongue cut out and his mouth closed to avoid the temptation of succulent fruits."

"Why have some cut off their feet?" Martala asked.

"To walk, to run, to dance, is to revel in the strength of the body, which is deemed sinful by our teachings."

"What about you?" I said. "Your face and body are intact."

"Not so." He slid his arms from his sleeves, and I saw that they ended in stumps. He had no hands.

"The sensation of touch is most alluring. I declined to allow it to anchor my soul to this earth."

"Very commendable of you," I said. If he perceived the scorn in my voice, he gave no sign.

He left us in a chamber full of steam that housed a row of copper tubs large enough to sit in. Two brothers of the sect filled three of these tubs with water that was heated on a stove at one end of the room. Both men were missing their ears, and the openings to where their ears had been were sewn shut. One was also missing his nose.

Other monks were bathing in several of the tubs. They walked through the room naked to get towels with which to dry themselves. One who had no feet crawled.

"Do you notice anything about those monks?" I said to Martala.

She glanced at them as she was removing her tunic. "What should I notice?"

"Each of them is missing some body part. But there is one organ of their bodies they all still possess."

She looked again, and nodded. "I think you are correct. That must be one sensation these madmen do not wish to sacrifice. But I see no women about."

"Perhaps they are all sodomites. I have been told it is not unusual in houses of religion."

"It's not our affair," she said with a shrug.

It was blissful to sink into hot, clean water after a dozen days of sweat, mud and biting insects. Martala said nothing, but I believe she enjoyed it. She showed not the least modesty in stripping down to her skin before me, but I expected otherwise from Anisah. I was mistaken. The girl was as quick to make herself naked as the Egyptian. It seemed that I was the only one of our party with any modesty. I hid my manhood in my hand as I stepped into the bath, and did the same thing stepping out. Monks came forward silently with white cotton towels to dry us. I wondered idly what had become of Martala's dagger, and decided she must have hidden it inside a folded towel.

Two monks approached with our clothing on their extended arms. I was astonished to see that the tunics, undershirts and pants were not only clean, but dry. We had been in the bath chamber no more than an hour, scarcely long enough to wash and dry clothes. Even our boots were dry and brushed clean of mud. As we stood dressing, the handless monk entered and stood in his usual posture, waiting. I looped the grass rope of my mace around my waist and tied it in place, feeling a bit foolish as I did so. It was a poor weapon. I wondered why the monks had not taken it away?

"If you will follow me, I will guide you to Worshipful Master," he said. "He is ready to receive you."

Chapter Fourteen

e followed the monk though dimly lit halls and along corridors. I was struck by the unnatural quiet of the building. Our boots striking the black-and-white tiled floors were by far the loudest sound. Monks paced past us like silent ghosts. Their long yellow robes concealed their feet, making them almost seem to glide along. The exceptions were those who had no feet, or no legs. All were mutilated in one way or another, most of them on their faces. One monk, who could not have been older than sixteen, felt his way along the wall. I saw that his sunken eye sockets were sewn shut. None of the monks spoke to us, or to each other. Those who could see avoided eye contact. The effect was disturbing.

"May I ask a question?" I said to our guide.

"Of course," he said without turning his head. "What is it you wish to know?"

"The Abbot Nicodemus said you were alchemists. I smell no sulfur. I hear no bellows. Where are your furnaces?"

"We practice a different kind of alchemy from that of the Christian brothers at the Soumela Monastery. Our alchemy is internal."

"Do you mean inside your bodies?"

"Yes. Our stove is the heat in our bellies. Our bellows are our lungs. Blood and flesh constitute our working materials."

"It's not really alchemy, then, is it?" Martala said.

He deigned to glance over his shoulder at her. "With it we distill the elixir."

"You don't make gold?"

"We have no use for gold."

Before we could question him at greater length, he led us through an open archway into an enormous square chamber in the center of which was a raised dais that was heaped with yellow silk cushions. The walls of the great room were bereft of tapestries or other hangings, and no carpets covered the polished black stones of its floor. But the strangest thing about the chamber was its lack of a ceiling. In one corner a flight of stone steps led up the side of the wall, then across the adjoining wall at a higher level, and so on, wrapping itself around the upper reaches of the space in a kind of squarish spiral that vanished into darkness far above. I realized we must be standing at the base of the tower we had seen as we approached the house of the Shenghuo.

Something pink squirmed amid the cushions on the dais, drawing my gaze to it for the first time. It was rounded and irregular in shape. I stared at it for a moment before I realized it possessed a shaved head. The ears and nose had been amputated and their holes sewn up, and the eye sockets sewn shut, presumably after removal of the eyes. The mouth was also sewn closed apart from a kind of pipe that projected from it. The thing shifted again, and I saw that it had no arms or legs. It was the naked torso of a human being. Even its manhood had been removed.

Behind it stood a young monk whose eyes and ears had been sewn shut. He held a flask of oil in one hand, and bent to apply it with his other hand to the undulating skin of the creature, which I could not think of in my own mind as a man.

"You will lie down with your foreheads touching the floor and your arms extended forward, as an expression of respect," the monk who was our escort told us.

I glanced at Martala. She nodded. Reluctantly, I did as instructed, but my cheeks flushed with hot blood at having to lower my dignity to something that was no longer human. If the Egyptian woman felt the same revulsion, she gave no sign of it. Anisah seemed unmoved by the sight, which surprised me given her sensitive nature. I reflected that perhaps she perceived more about the monster than was evident to me.

"Stand now. Exalted Master will speak with you."

The obvious question arose in my mind, but I held my tongue. The monk turned and walked out. We looked at each other, then back at the pink blob on the dais. There was no one else in the vast, silent space apart from the monk applying oil to its body.

"I welcome the four of you to our humble house of learning, brave companions of Abdul Alhazred," Anisah said in a clear voice. She was staring at the pink thing, and seemed to be in a kind of trance.

"Are you speaking through the girl?" Martala asked.

"Obviously, and hearing with her ears."

"Can you see us?"

"I see you through the eyes of Anisah, a most remarkable young woman."

I turned from Anisah to Martala in confusion. "Is that thing controlling her?"

"Calm yourself, Hassid, I mean you no harm."

"If you hurt the girl I will kill you." I unwound my crude mace from my waist and cradled its stone in my hand.

"You would find that impossible. But trust me when I say that none of you will be harmed in my house."

"Why did you wish to bring us here?" Martala asked.

"I was curious when I learned about the girl. She is not completely human."

"Her mother is the queen of a djinn-like race that dwells on an isle far to the west beyond the Pillars of Hercules," Martala said.

"She has extraordinary gifts."

"Do you mean her intuition and ability to sense things? I presume that is why you chose her to communicate with us."

The thing on the dais wagged its smooth head from side to side, causing the young monk to pause his application of the oil.

"She possesses latent powers that are beyond anything either of you can begin to imagine. The Greeks would call her a demi-god."

"So that is why Brother Lucius is so eager to gain possession of her."

"Correct. He thinks he can control her and learn to exploit her abilities for his own purposes. He is a fool, as I am sure you yourselves have already observed."

"Do you intend to hold her here for your purposes?" Martala asked.

"That is not our way. You are all free to depart at any moment you choose. It is only a question of which way you will go."

"I seek to recover the mortal remains of Alhazred, wherever they may lie."

"Remains?" There was a note of puzzlement in Anisah's voice. "Ah, I perceive your thoughts. You believe the necromancer was killed."

I stared at the monster, than at Martala. Her ice-blue eyes widened.

"His death was a theatrical performance, nothing more. I gather from your surprise that it was quite convincing."

"Tell me clearly," Martala said in a low, slow voice. "Are you saying that Alhazred still lives?"

"That is what I am saying."

"Where? Where is he?" She could scarcely contain the rise in her voice.

The pink lump of flesh shifted on its cushions with a ripple of the muscles beneath its skin. "I was commanded to arrange the deception you witnessed in the Damascus market square, and to convey Alhazred to this chamber."

"Do you have him here?" she asked with excitement. "Is he your captive?"

"No. He was taken from us."

"Where was he taken?"

"As to that, I cannot be certain. My mind will not reach beyond the bounds of this world."

"You are saying he was taken to another world?"

"Another world, another realm, another dimension of space. These words are poor tools and fail to describe the reality. Let me say only to you that he was taken elsewhere."

Anisah raised her right hand and pointed upward at the darkness in the belly of the tower.

"You mean he was taken up those stairs?"

"Yes."

"Then the tower is a portal."

"Of a kind."

"I must go to him at once."

"Of course you must. No one will try to stop you. But first, I ask that you converse with me a while longer. I so seldom have occasion to talk to such amusing visitors, and you four are quite diverting in your several ways."

She frowned with impatience. I made a warning gesture with my hand and spoke to prevent her saying something rash.

"There are only three of us."

The pink blob rippled. I realized it must be silently laughing. Its attendant stopped applying the oil until it was still.

"Your mind is twofold now, Hassid. I perceive you have a djinn of the desert spaces dwelling within you. Such an unusual choice for a traveling companion."

"It was less a choice than a necessity," Martala said.

"It was Alhazred's companion," I explained. "I carry it in his stead."

"I see the way of it now. Your loyalty to your teacher is commendable."

"From your speech, you appear to be an enlightened being," I said. "Why have you allied your sect with the monks of Soumela? You must know that they are murderers and cannibals."

"We all serve someone, or something. The Order of Ambrose worships the same god to whom our sect owes its service. We fulfill its purposes on your world from time to time in return for various considerations of an esoteric nature done on our behalf. The monks are our instruments, nothing more."

"You have renounced the world and its sensations. What consideration can be so important that you would lower yourself to commit such base deception?"

"Our lives are devoted to the acquisition of knowledge," it said with a tilt of its head. "Our greatest enemy has always been time. We need time to read, time to think, time to question, and time to seek answers in strange and distant lands. But human life is so brief."

"Your god gave you a way to extend your lives," she said with sudden understanding.

"The greatest gift to seekers of knowledge, time itself. For that we serve the purposes of the one who commands us."

"We were informed that you worship Yog-Sothoth," Martala said.

"That is not quite accurate. We commune through Yog-Sothoth, who is all gateways, and make use of his portals, but our devotion is given to the Dweller Beyond the Threshold."

"Of whom do you speak? Is it—?"

"Do not speak his name," Anisah said sharply with an edge of command in her voice. "No, he is not the one we serve."

"Then tell me this, why did your god order that Alhazred be abducted?"

"The necromancer sought to steal knowledge through the use of certain invisible agents. That knowledge is not permitted to be possessed except by those who have paid the required price of its possession."

"Do you mean your physical disfigurement?"

The pink thing rippled.

"These amputations from our bodies are of no great consequence. The price asked for the knowledge Alhazred sought is considerably greater. He tried to steal that knowledge from the Dweller, and he was punished for his hubris."

"By the demon that tore his body to pieces."

"It did not dismember him. That was merely a glamour to deceive onlookers and persuade them he was dead. The demon, as you call it, carried him from Damascus to this very chamber, where he was given over into the keeping of the servants of the one who wishes to punish him for eternity."

"Is he being tortured?"

"To be sure. I believe his agonies must be exquisite. In a sense, I envy him, to be able to experience such intense sensation not only with the body but with the mind as well. Few beings in this world or any other have known such transcendent pain."

The expression on Martala's face turned to pure fury. I thought for a moment she would leap upon the dais and slay the little monster with her dagger, but she did not move so much as a finger.

"Will you tell us what dangers lie before us at the top of the tower?"

There was a pause in Anisah's speech. "I think not. I think I will allow you the delight of experiencing them for yourselves, with untainted minds."

"Then you are useless to us," Martala said, a savage note in her voice. "Keep your monks out of our way if you want them to continue living."

The pink thing rippled. "I will release the mind of the girl. This has been a most diverting experience very much worth waiting for. You have my sincere thanks for providing it."

Martala went to Anisah and shook her by the shoulders. The girl blinked several times and gazed around her with an empty expression. Her eyes fell upon the pink thing and her face hardened in anger.

"You violated me. Do not try it again, or you will regret it."

The threat was spoken in a quiet voice but something in the words felt like iron. It was almost as if some other intelligence were speaking, one that was greater and more remote than that of the girl, yet still a part of her.

The thing on the dais flinched back at her words and almost fell over. I realized it must have heard her words without ears, or otherwise sensed them. It began to quiver in agitation.

"Let's go before it summons its monks and has us all killed," I murmured to Martala.

"I've not seen a single weapon in this damned place," she said. "We need weapons."

"I have this." I held up my rock.

In spite of herself, she gave a short laugh. "We're going up those stairs, weapons or not. Alhazred is alive. That is more than I ever dared to hope for, or even to dream possible. I won't stop searching until I find him and free him."

"Then let us go together," I said.

Chapter Fifteen

We began to climb. Before we had gone a single flight of steps, I heard the patter of tiny bare feet on the floor and looked behind.

The homunculus reached the bottom of the stair and laboriously began to pull himself up it, one step at a time. This was awkward, since the steps came up almost to his waist.

"What are you doing?" Martala demanded.

"I'm coming with you."

"I thought you had tasks to perform," I said.

"I'm tired of being a slave. Wherever you are going, it's away from here."

"It couldn't be that Enlightened Master told you to accompany us, so that you can watch us and report what we do?" Martala said.

The little man made no answer. He continued to pull himself up one step at a time, a look of concentration on his face.

"Let him come," Anisah said.

"Why? Do you foresee something?"

"No. But I have a feeling that he may prove useful."

"That's good enough for me," I said to Martala.

"So be it. But I don't trust him."

"Can you open portals?" I asked the homunculus.

"Not between worlds. But from place to place."

"What is your name, little man? If you are coming with us, we need to call you something."

He stopped and looked at me. "I lied to you before. I don't have a name." He said the words as if realizing their full truth for the first time.

"Then what do you want to be called?"

"I don't know. It is not something I've ever considered." He pointed at Anisah. "She can name me."

We waited while Anisah considered. "I will name you Kanenas."

"What kind of a name is Kanenas?" the homunculus demanded.

"Come on," Martala said with impatience. "If we stand here any longer, the monks may shoot us down with bows."

I looked down. There did not appear to be any activity on the floor below. None of the monks were present. The dais itself was empty. They must have carried off their lump of a Master as we began our climb.

"Kanenas, if you are to walk with us, you must obey my orders," Martala said. "Unless you agree, you cannot come with us."

"I agree, I agree," Kanenas said. "Now let's get away from this place before the Master calls me back with his mind."

We resumed the climb. The stone stairs projected from the four walls of the tower. There was no outer railing, and they were less than two cubits wide, so we hugged the wall to prevent a misstep, which would have been fatal. Martala went first, then Anisah, then me, and the little man came behind, grunting and huffing with the effort of the climb.

Soon the floor of the tower far below was a small patch of light. There was only darkness above and on all sides. We climbed by touch. Martala went cautiously, for there was no way to know if the stairs would suddenly end in the blackness, which became absolute. My legs began to ache. I almost felt pity for Kanenas, but the little man never complained, probably because he knew it would accomplish nothing. The stairs seemed endless. I soon lost track of how many times we wound around the four sides of the tower.

After what seemed several hours of climbing, we stopped to rest our legs. I sat on a step with my arms across my knees, breathing heavily. I heard Kanenas sit down beside me on the outer edge of the step.

"You know we are probably climbing to our deaths," I said.

"I know," he said in his shrill voice.

"Then why come with us? You could have crossed the plateau and escaped that way."

"Alone? The hounds would have eaten me on the first day."

"You can make portals through space. Make a portal to Damascus, or Cappadocia, or anywhere away from this place."

"I cannot make portals for my own use, only for the use of others."

I thought for a moment. "I could tell you to make me a portal to Cappadocia, and then you could step through it while I stayed behind."

"It wouldn't work. I would know it was a trick."

"Is there nowhere you want to go? No one you wish to be with?"

"I have no one, and nothing," he said without self-pity. "I am a made thing, to be used and then unmade."

In spite of my better judgment, I felt a stirring of sympathy for the strange little creature. It was a terrible thing to have no family, no ancestors, no friends, no companion. What would be the point of living?

We resumed the climb. The spot of light at the bottom of the stairs was no longer visible when I leaned over the edge and looked down, but there was nothing above but blackness. The dark seemed to press in upon me from all sides, as though it were the soft, sable pelt of a living creature. When I thought about it, I found it hard to breathe, so I forced it out of my mind and concentrated on my legs, which screamed for relief. My thighs felt as though they were on fire, and my feet hurt every time I pressed them down on the stones of the steps. I heard the labored breathing of my companions.

"The tower cannot possibly be this high," I said.

"It must have an enchantment on it," Martala said.

"If that is so, then we may be climbing for eternity. We will starve to death on these stairs."

"Not so," she said. "We will die of thirst long before we starve to death."

"That's a comfort, I suppose."

"Do you regret coming with me?"

I thought for a moment. "Of course I regret coming with you. I could be at home in my father's house, drinking wine and eating grapes while a servant girl rubbed my feet. I would have to be insane not to regret coming with you."

Anisah laughed. It was a light, musical sound that for a moment pushed back the press of darkness from my face. Then the black returned.

Something brushed my cheek. I felt a sharp pain and batted it away. It made a faint squeak.

Martala cursed. "Bats. Protect your eyes."

Soon they were all around us. Their wings were almost silent as they flew, but they emitted squeaks that were heard when they came close. I could see nothing but guessed there must be dozens of the creatures, all seeking a piece of my flesh. They bit my scalp, my neck, my hands as I tried to knock them away. Kanenas cried out and then kept up a steady stream of curses in Greek that enlarged my vocabulary of that language. The women seemed less affected, perhaps because they had head coverings.

I caught one of the things in my hand. It bit my thumb but I held onto it. The body of the creature was not covered with fur like a bat, but felt smooth and segmented, and it had many legs. Its wings buzzed against my hand. I squeezed harder until it ceased to struggle, then cast it into space.

"They are not bats," I said.

"What then?" Martala asked.

"I don't know, but not bats."

In spite of the assault we continued to mount the stairs.

After a while the attacks became less vexing, and then ceased. I had been bitten at least a dozen times. Each bite twinged as though a hot needle were inserted there. From this I concluded that the bites were poisonous. I waited for them to numb my body and stop my heart, but they seemed to only cause pain.

"We must have passed their hunting zone," I said after nothing had bitten me for several minutes.

"The vicious creatures tried to pick me up and carry me off," Kanenas said in a tone of outrage, then laughed. "They will regret it. They did not know that my blood is poison."

As we climbed, I noticed that the flights of steps along each wall of the tower seemed shorter than the flights nearer the bottom. I mentioned this impression to Martala.

"You are correct, Hassid," she said. "I have been counting the steps in each flight. Every so often the number is reduced by one."

"That means the tower is narrowing," I said. "When we saw it from the outside, I remember it was narrower at the top than at the bottom."

Once the matter had been plainly stated, it became obvious. Each flight of steps was a little shorter than the previous flight. This was done by narrowing the width of the treads. After nine flights, the number of steps in a flight was reduced by one, and the remaining treads returned to their original width, only to successively narrow again as we continued upward, until the next step was removed.

There was another change. Although I could see nothing, the darkness pressing around me seemed closer, tighter in some way, the higher we climbed. The echo of our voices from the walls ceased. To my mind, this indicated a narrowing of the tower.

When it seemed that we had been climbing forever, and I was about to beg Martala to call a halt so that we could sleep, I saw something above us that made my heart leap with hope.

"Stars!" I said. "Look up, there are stars."

Above in the blackness was a small square speckled with points of light. It looked like a black scarf with grains of salt scattered across it.

"Praise be to Yog-Sothoth," Kanenas said. "I was ready to throw myself off the edge."

I said nothing in response, but inwardly I suspected all of us would have reached the same state of mind, had the stair continued much longer.

We climbed toward the stars. At some point I chanced to reach out my hand over the edge of the steps, and felt the tips of my fingers brush against stone. With care, I felt the thing I had touched, and realized it was the end of another flight of stairs. The tower had narrowed to such a degree, I was able to touch the other side. There were now no more than a handful of steps in each flight.

At last, our climb came to an end. We emerged one by one from a square hole no more than four or five cubits across that was surrounded by a low stone wall. It projected up from a flat surface paved with stones. At first I could make no sense of what we were standing on. The light from the stars was dim, but my eyes were long adapted to darkness, allowing me to trace the outlines of shapes. I looked around the vast open space and saw distant buildings that towered above us. I reeled and almost fell, so great was the shock of understanding.

We had emerged from the mouth of a well onto the plaza of some strange city of giants. Its buildings stood like mountain cliffs on every side. I had never seen any structure built by human hands that reached so high. Their tops seemed to brush the very stars. All these cyclopean works were unilluminated, so I could not tell if they contained windows. They were no more than oblong blocks of shadow against the starlight. The silence was absolute. I wondered if the buildings had been abandoned.

"We are in some kind of city," Martala said softly.

Taking care, I leaned over the side of the well and peered down into its depths. To my surprise I saw a floor of what looked like polished obsidian. It reflected the stars. I reached into the well and was able to brush it with my fingertips.

"We cannot go back," I said.

Martala leaned over the wall of the well and peered down. She straightened and looked all around. "We're too exposed here in the open; we need to find concealment."

We crossed the vast plaza, larger by far than any in Damascus, and approached one of the towering dark structures at its edge. By the dim starlight I discerned an oblong outline in the side of it. As we drew near, I saw that this vast rectangle was recessed into the stone of the building, and its edge was ornamented with a kind of geometric border.

I could imagine no possible purpose for this recess, and was about to dismiss it from my thoughts when it silently opened.

Chapter Sixteen

ight spilled out the opening in the wall, blinding me. We quickly cowered back to one side of the doorway, for such it evidently was, although larger by far than any door I had ever seen. The light was not the yellow of a lantern flame, but all the colors of the rainbow. They mingled and flashed against one another in a way that dazzled my vision and hurt my head. I held onto the wall to keep from falling.

Something came forth from the doorway. I felt its massive body moving past us through the darkness. A kind of heat radiated from it that made the skin on my face prickle. I strained my watering eyes but I saw nothing in the dim starlight. Nor was there any sound of footfalls. The giant thing seemed to float upon the air, and was invisible.

The door slid down silently, blocking the crazed rainbow. The dizziness in my head began to go away. I blinked in an effort to clear the colored spots that persisted in my eyes.

"That must be what lives in these buildings," I murmured.

"Whatever it was, it was big," Martala said. She looked down at Kanenas, who was cowering behind Anisah, his arms around her leg. "Do you know what it was?"

The homunculus released the girl and stood trembling with fear. "I only know that its race is favored by Yog-Sothoth. That is why the Shenghuo Sect have a pact with its kind. The Master receives alchemical knowledge from them, and in return, he serves their obscure purposes on our world, or rather, the purposes of their master. But this is the first time I have ever been close to one."

"What kind of knowledge?" she asked.

"Secrets having to do with the curing of infirmities. The prolongation of life. The restoration of the dead to the world of the living."

"That last secret has been known for centuries."

"Indeed. Where did you think it originated?"

"You mean this race of invisible giants gave it to men."

The little man nodded.

"How are we to find Alhazred, if he is being held a prisoner by such monsters?" I asked.

"We look," Martala said. Her tone made me hold my tongue.

We wandered through the wide avenues of the dark city. Nowhere was there a light from a window or a doorway. We might have taken it to be a city of the dead but for our recent encounter with one of its inhabitants. The air smelled strange. It left a metallic taint on my tongue and a slight burning in my lungs. For miles we crept between the vast towers, which were of geometrical designs, with sharp corners, cones, and rounded domes, all constructed from the same seamless black rock. I realized the rock was similar, if not identical, to the black slabs that formed the house of the Shenghuo Sect.

"This is getting us nowhere," the little man said when we had walked for hours. "My legs are tired. I want to find a nice fire where I can curl up and go to sleep."

I found myself mentally agreeing with Kanenas, but did not speak. Martala's temper was at the edge of explosion. It was evident in the way she moved, the glare in her eyes. She wanted to kill something.

Before Kanenas could get himself into trouble by speaking again, we came upon a strange structure that was completely out of keeping with the colossal architecture of the dark city. At the base of one of the towering walls was a kind of tube made of mud. It looked tiny, but as we drew nearer I saw that it was higher than my head. It had been plastered into the angle where the vertical wall met the flat surface of the roadway. I wondered what strange creatures had created it. The roundness of its construction reminded me of nests made by wasps. At the end of this earthen tube was a circular opening covered by what appeared to be an animal skin of some kind.

We stopped a little distance away, undecided.

"Whatever lives in there may be hostile, or hungry," Martala said. Her dagger was in her hand.

"We should not disturb it," Kanenas said.

She shook her head. "I need to learn where Alhazred is being held, if he is still in this world."

She approached the opening cautiously, her weapon held in front of her, and reached to tug on the leather cover. Before her fingers touched, it was flung aside, and we were confronted by a woman who glared at us. Her long hair was tied behind her head. She wore a kind of dress made of the same leather that formed the door.

We stared at each other in silence for a time.

"What place do you come from?" she asked in broken Greek.

"Damascus," I said.

"You better come inside. There's food and a fire."

I looked at Martala, who hesitated. The alien woman never knew how close she came to death.

"We should go in," Anisah said. "There is no danger here."

Martala shrugged, and bent to climb through the round doorway. The girl went after her. Swallowing my misgivings, I followed, and the little man came after me.

Inside the tunnel the odor was strong but familiar. It was the scent of many human beings living together without regular bathing. There were also cooking smells. Several clay oil lamps gave a yellow glow. I saw by their light that the hair of our escort was dark red. An old woman with wild white locks that tumbled over her skinny shoulders glanced up from a smokeless fire she was tending with a bone that looked very much like a human rib. She grinned, showing the gaps between her blackened teeth. Over the embers hung what looked like flatbread. In a clay pot bubbled a kind of soup or stew. Other men and women drew nearer from the depths of the tunnel to stare at us. There was no hostility in their eyes, but in the gaze of a few I thought I detected pity.

"How do so many human beings come to be in this strange world?" Martala demanded.

"The same way you came here," the woman said. "The gates of Yog-Sothoth opened."

"Your accent is unfamiliar to me."

"I come from the land of Britannia, which the Romans called Albion. It is an island—"

"I know where Albion is," Martala said with impatience. "Can you open a portal back to our world?"

Several of those who had gathered to listen laughed, but there was no mirth in their laughter.

"Do you think any of us would still be here if we could go back?"

"Then why did you come here?"

"By accident. By misadventure. Some were carried against their will to be experimented upon by the Old Ones."

"The Old Ones?"

"Haven't you met them yet? That's probably why you are still alive. They usually kill our kind on sight."

Martala looked around. "All of you are still alive."

"We are so small to them, they usually don't notice us unless we move or try to run away," a man said. "Then, *zat!*" He made a striking motion with his hand. Several others nodded.

"They throw lightning bolts," the red-haired Briton explained.

"Why do you stay in their city?"

Again, several chuckled in a rueful tone.

"We tried to leave," the woman said. "This city has no end. We walked for weeks. It was still all paved streets and tall buildings. So we came back."

"How do you survive?" I asked. "Where do you get your food?"

"We use what the Old Ones discard," the old woman said, still stirring the embers of her smokeless fire in its clay fireplace.

"When things fall from their bodies, they become visible," the red-haired woman explained. "Our clothing is made of their skins, which they periodically shed. Our fire comes from what we suppose must be their dung. After they shit, it glows with heat and light due to some internal property. We are not the only vermin infesting this city that fell through the gates of Yog-Sothoth. There are rats, lizards, snakes. We eat the flesh of what we can catch and kill. Most of our diet comes from a kind of fungi we cultivate in the depths of our tunnels."

"There are more tunnels like this one?"

"A few. The others hunt us for our flesh, so we keep our distance."

"Where do you get your water?" I asked.

"It rains every few days. We collect it in earthen pots."

"I saw no clay with which to make pots," Martala said.

"We dig for it," a man said. There was a scar running across his face and through one of his eye sockets. The eye was missing.

"We came here through a well that lies not far from this place in an open square," Martala said. "You can get to the Plateau of Leng if you are able to climb down it."

Several people who heard her words laughed bitterly.

"We've tried all the wells," the red-haired woman said. "They are sealed."

"It is a one-way portal," the little man told Martala. "It brought you here, but unless Yog-Sothoth chooses to open it, you cannot use it to go back."

"Come, sit and eat," the woman said. "There is ample time for your questions later. That is one thing we have more than enough of in this accursed city—time."

The flatbread, which I assumed must have been made from the cultivated fungi, was surprisingly good to eat. A man brought forth a vessel that contained a fermented liquid that tasted somewhat like beer. The little man's aversion to water did not extend to this alcoholic beverage. He drank more than his share of it, and after a time became talkative. He even sang a song in some strange language I did not recognize. The natives of this world, as I thought of these stranded wayfarers, were surprisingly lacking in interest concerning his appearance, and paid just as little heed to his words. Indeed, there was a general dullness, or listlessness, about them all.

We were given sleeping mats of the same stiff leather, and all but one of the lamps was extinguished. The entrance to the tunnel was blocked with stones. We lay down on the mats, and the homunculus climbed into the embers of the fireplace, which showed no signs of burning out, and curled himself up on them to sleep.

"Do you think they are cannibals?" I whispered to Martala, who lay next to me.

"It would not be surprising. Meat must be hard to find."

"Anisah felt no hostility from them."

"I still don't trust them."

"I wish I had my sword."

"If wishes were camels, beggars would ride."

"Or even my dagger."

"Go to sleep, Hassid."

Chapter Seventeen

reakfast the following morning was made up of the leftover flatbread from the previous evening. The tunnel dwellers moved about in a listless manner, doing the necessary tasks required to keep their small community functioning. My companions and I were permitted to freely observe them and question them. We were not the first group of travelers to stumble upon them, so our presence aroused no excitement. They had answered the same questions many times and were obviously indifferent to our reactions.

"Why are there no children?" Martala asked the Celtic woman with the red hair, whose name was Boacia.

"We don't know. Children are conceived, but they are always stillborn mid-term. Maybe it's something in the air, or the water, or the food we eat. We don't know."

She said it without emotion. I wondered if she had suffered one of these stillbirths? If so, it was not a memory that aroused strong feeling in her. Perhaps she had buried it so deeply that it could no longer touch her. She sat weaving a rope from strips of the leather that was the cast-off hide of an invisible giant.

"They mostly travel across the city at night," the one-eyed man with the scar told me when I asked about them. His name was Tolli. "Mostly, mind you. If you keep still and stand near a wall when they pass, chances are they won't kill you."

"A good thing to know," I said. "Are there many of them?"

"No. The city is vast, but they are few. Or at least, only a few venture out of their buildings. The danger lies in stumbling into one on the street when you are walking. They seldom make any sounds, but you can tell when they are close by the warmth that radiates from their bodies."

"I've felt it."

"It's like the heat of the sun, or the heat from this fire where your little friend is sleeping. It makes the skin on your face tingle. When they are about to hurl a bolt of lightning, they make a crackling noise, like the rustle of dry leaves."

"Are there any other dangers?"

"Vermin. Most are no bigger than dogs and easily killed with knives or stones. They flee from our kind. The monsters keep a slave race that does their work for them. You should avoid them at all costs. But they only come out at night."

"What do they look like?"

"They are black all over, hard to see in the dark, and their bodies are covered with a kind of shell-like substance. I think they look like insects although they walk on two legs. They stand taller than a man. When they see our race they try to capture us with nets, and if they succeed they take us away."

"What happens to those who are taken?"

He shrugged. "No one has seen. If I had to guess I would say they are tortured, slaughtered and eaten."

"Are the men going to unblock the doorway soon? I feel the need to relieve myself."

"They are just doing it now. We wait until the sun is well up in the sky before going out. Most of the more dangerous vermin return to their dens during the day."

A man and a boy of about fourteen years removed the stones from the mouth of the tunnel and piled them to either side to be used the next evening. To my surprise, very little light entered.

I crouched and went out through the low opening, then straightened and looked around. At first I thought it was still night, and that the tunnel dwellers were playing some joke on me, but then I realized that it was brighter than it had been the night before. A kind of dull red glow lit the road's surface and the featureless walls of the buildings that towered above me on either side.

I looked down along the street and saw a red ball hanging in the dark sky. It was much larger than the sun of my world, and the color of soot-covered embers. It gave so little light that the brighter stars were visible around it. None the less, I felt warmth on my face radiating down from it, like the warmth that goes forth from heated iron.

"A black sun," Anisah said as she came forth to stand beside me.

"Even the days here are night."

"At least it's warm. I can feel it prickling on my arms and face."

"It's like the heat from the embers in the fireplace," I said. "There is something unnatural about it that I don't like."

Martala stepped forth, followed by Kanenas, who scowled at us and yawned.

"Boacia tells me there is a large building in the middle of a great plaza a few miles from here, in the direction of the rising sun, where the Old Ones sometimes gather. I'm going to go and see if there is any evidence that Alhazred was kept there."

"We'll go with you," I said, looking at Anisah and Kanenas. The little man scowled, than reluctantly nodded.

"I was able to trade my tinderbox for this." She held up a long bone that had been sharpened on one end. It looked to me like a thighbone from a human being. She gave it to me. I slid it under my belt. The bony knob at the end kept it from falling out.

"I don't like the way the sun feels," Anisah said, looking around her. "There is a sickness in the air. All those people inside the tunnel are sick. They are dying."

"When we find Alhazred and set him free, he will get us back to our own world," Martala said.

"You have great confidence in the abilities of this necromancer," Kanenas said with skepticism in his voice.

"Yes, I do," Martala said.

"If he is so powerful, why did he allow himself to be abducted?"

This was a new thought to me. What if Alhazred had not been captured against his will, but had foreseen his fate and had allowed himself to be taken? I pondered on this but could think of no sane reason why he would wish to come to this evil place.

We set out in the direction of the rising sun, weaving our way cautiously between the monolithic towers of stone, with their strange shapes and uncouth angles. Some leaned over us and looked as if they were about to fall and crush us. Others formed bridges across the broad avenues, and we walked under their bulks with cautious steps, trying to make as little sound as possible. Tolli had told me the Old Ones mostly traveled abroad in the night, but he had not said always. Now and then some small creature peeked at us around a corner, then dashed away.

"There is something ahead," Martala whispered.

I strained my eyes in the dim light and saw a great mass of shadow that loomed up beyond the walls of the buildings.

The road we followed ended on the largest open plaza I had ever seen. In the midst of it stood a black pyramid of almost incomprehensible vastness.

"It's bigger than the Pyramid of Cheops at Memphis," Martala said.

"You've seen the Great Pyramid of Egypt?" I asked.

"I've climbed to the top of it."

I had only seen drawings of the great Egyptian pyramid, which was more squat than this black pyramid that rose above us like the obsidian point of a spear. Its apex reached much higher into the heavens than any other structure of the city.

There was a blinding flash of white light followed almost immediately by a loud crack that echoed like thunder and made us all flinch backwards and shield our faces with our arms. A bolt of lightning had lanced upward from the needle-like point of the pyramid. I blinked and saw it still, burned into my eyes. It was some while before it began to fade from my vision.

"Look there," Anisah said, pointing. Still blinking tears from my eyes, I saw that a black sphere rested in the plaza near the pyramid, which did not appear to have any openings of any kind.

"I have seen something like that before, on a floating island in the Red Sea," Martala said.

She started across the plaza toward the sphere. I hesitated for a moment, then followed with nervous glances over my shoulders to see if anything was watching us. The city might as well have been a necropolis. We were the only ones moving through it.

Martala stopped in front of the sphere and waited for us. Although it was dwarfed by the pyramid, it towered above us, a featureless black that did not reflect the stars. When I drew near, I realized that by some magic it floated just above the paving stones without touching them.

"If you are afraid to follow, stay here and wait for me," Martala said.

I was about to ask what she meant when she turned and stepped into the sphere as though it were a patch of shadow.

"It's a portal, fool," Kanenas said to me with contempt. He went forward and passed into the sphere.

Anisah looked at me nervously. I took her hand in mine. Her fingers were cool and dry.

"We'll go in together," I said, trying to make my voice confident.

She smiled and nodded. Together we stepped into the blackness.

Chapter Eighteen

We found ourselves within a dimly lit chamber with a vaulted ceiling that towered high above us. It was enormous, a room made for the floating giants. Kanenas stood watching me with amusement. Martala held her dagger in her hand.

"Where are we?" I asked.

"Inside the pyramid, where else?" Kanenas said. "The sphere is its doorway, or one of them."

"We must move with caution," Martala said. "If we are seen, we will be captured and tortured. I know the alien race that uses black spheres. Alhazred and I fought it many years ago, and drove it off our world."

"Are they the black-shelled creatures that look like insects Tolli told me about?"

She nodded at me. We followed close on her heels as she crept forward across the vaulted chamber, which was lined on either side with standing figures in stone and metal that must have been sculptures, although some of them were so ill-formed, they did not even resemble living creatures.

"What dealings did you and Alhazred have with this insect race?" I murmured.

"They came on a floating island and enslaved the mariners whose vessels wrecked on its stony reefs. They are necromancers with the power to revive the dead, not as we do from their essential salts, but as walking corpses without souls. They used the dead as workers to build a fortress on their island. We caused the island to destroy itself, and all the insect things with it. I never thought to see their kind again in this lifetime."

"What are they doing on this world?" Anisah asked.

"Tolli called them a slave race that does the work of the Old Ones," I said.

"They are skillful builders, and use many strange weapons and tools," Martala said. "Beware of a silver tube they carry. It shoots death."

We passed through chambers that were filled with strange glass vessels connected by glass tubes, in which bubbled a green liquid. Some of these vessels were over flames that boiled their contents and sent the steam through the tubes, to be condensed elsewhere in the form of green droplets. It was a kind of alchemy, that much was plain, but I could make no sense of it. The smell was vile.

All of the workrooms through which we passed were deserted, but some appeared to have been vacated only minutes earlier. Various alchemical processes were still ongoing on the work tables, the flames still burning beneath vessels, the furnaces still glowing. The reason for their emptiness suggested itself when we heard a kind of droning of many alien voices from somewhere ahead.

"They must be gathered together for some religious ritual," I said.

We followed the sound and came to an archway that opened upon a great chamber that was so wide and lofty, it almost felt like the outer world. In its general shape it was similar to the audience chamber of Exalted Master of the Shenghuo Sect on the Plateau of Leng, but it was many times larger. Countless glowing orbs set in its walls provided a red light that cast no shadows. The only darkness was above, where the tapering walls converged on a patch of black far overhead.

At the far side of this cavernous chamber were gathered perhaps a hundred black-shelled slave creatures that resembled beetles or ants in the distance, save that they walked upright. Their legs were too long, and folded in a manner that was opposite to human legs.

The creatures had arrayed themselves in rows before a raised platform with a low back that resembled a kind of gargantuan chair. They had their backs to us. We moved behind the wall hangings, keeping out of sight most of the time, although none of them faced in our direction. One who was dressed in a resplendent robe of red and gold led the chanting. He, too, faced the empty chair. From time to time the creatures knelt and prostrated themselves upon the floor, buzzing and clicking in unison. They appeared to be engaged in devotion, but there was no statue or image to worship.

On either side, two of the beings controlled light projectors that cast a bright glow upon the great chair. They were machines with complex arrangements of mirrors and lamps and colored disks that caused the projected light to change color in a rhythmic way. We stood at the edge of one of the vast wall hangings and watched this incomprehensible activity.

"What are they doing?" Anisah whispered.

"It looked like some kind of worship," Martala said.

"Their god must be invisible, as ours is," I said.

"When I lived in Egypt my goddess was Baast, goddess of cats. I gave her statue my adoration, but I never groveled on the floor before her."

"They do so out of fear," Anisah said. "I can sense it."

"We should move on quickly," Kanenas said. "Someone may turn around."

"They aren't even facing this way. I want to watch," Martala told him.

The two insect creatures on either side of the great chair who worked the machines of projection caused the light shining from them to mingle in a rainbow of colors that flashed and sparkled. Suddenly the chair was no longer empty. Something huge sat or squatted on it. It was larger than any elephant I had ever seen. I stared at it, trying to make sense of its form. There were bulging protrusions on parts of its lumpy body, and appendages that swayed and undulated. As my mind fought with itself to understand their shapes, pain lanced through my head and I grew dizzy.

"Don't look at it," Kanenas said sharply. "Cover your eyes, if you value your sanity."

I did as he directed and felt tears on my cheeks. My eyes were streaming water. I pulled Martala and Anisah back behind the edge of the wall hanging, then had to catch the Egyptian woman in my arms as she stumbled.

"What's happening?" she said weakly.

"That thing in the chair; it must be one of the invisible monsters that live inside the buildings. The colored lights shining upon it rendered it visible to our eyes."

"Your eyes and your minds are not adapted to see such things," Kanenas said. "If you had looked any longer, it would have driven you all mad."

"I felt nothing," Anisah said.

I stared at her. She supported Martala by the arm, and seemed composed apart from her concern for the well-being of the other woman.

"You looked at the lights, and saw the monster?"

"Yes."

"And you felt nothing?"

She shook her head. "It is very ugly."

I looked at Martala, who shrugged. Something in Anisah's mixed heritage must be protecting her from the harmful effects of the colors.

"What of you, Kanenas?" I asked the little man.

"It hurts my head, but I can endure it for a short time."

I risked another glance around the edge of the hanging. The light machines had been tuned to simple red light, and the chair appeared empty once more. I wondered if the bloated monster that had squatted on it was still there, and was looking at me. Or did it even have eyes? I could not remember seeing any on its surface. The memory caused pain to lance through my brain once again and I turned my thoughts away from it.

The insect creatures were carrying in large jars, boxes and rolls of what looked like bolts of cloth. They piled them on the floor before the chair.

"Offerings to their god," Martala murmured. I realized she was peering over my shoulder.

After depositing their burdens, they moved quickly away to either side. I noticed that there was a circle engraved on the stone floor around the offerings.

A tone sounded from the vicinity of the chair. It was so deep, I felt it more than heard it. The richly robed insect creature who appeared to be leading the worship bowed low, if what it did with its misshapen body can even be called a bow, and gestured at the two others who worked the light machines. Once again the rainbow pattern of colors began to play over the chamber. Before I could close my eyes or pull my head back, I was blinded by a white flash that lanced down from the darkness of the ceiling, and at the same instant, a crashing roar deafened me. I fell backward, knocking Martala down with me.

We quickly picked ourselves up. My ears rang and my eyes were full of streaks of light that changed colors as I tried to blink them away. I forced myself to look around the hanging, and saw through my tears of pain that the offerings were no longer on the floor. In their place rested a single crystal vessel.

The robed priest came forward, bowed deeply, and used two of its appendages to pick up the crystal jar from the floor. It carried it reverently away while the gathered worshippers continued to buzz and click. The air stirred. Blinking rapidly, I tried to see what was going on past the colored blotches that had been burned into my eyes. Something had changed. A presence that had been there was missing.

"It's gone," Anisah said. "The invisible monster is no longer in this room."

The chanting ceased. The light machines were turned off, and the insect creatures climbed to their feet and began to file out through two archways behind the chair. A few came toward us, and we hid until they passed out the archway next to the hanging that gave us concealment.

"I don't think they have good eyesight," I said. "They should have seen us."

"We were foolish to come here," Kanenas grumbled. "It was far too dangerous. If they capture us they will torture us to learn who we are and then kill us."

"What did we see?" Martala asked.

"I see spots," I told her. "My ears are still ringing."

"It was lightning," Kanenas said. "Remember, we saw it strike the pyramid when we were outside it?"

"The offerings on the floor vanished, and were replaced by a crystalline jar of some kind," I said. "I think there was something in it."

"The lightning must be a portal," Kanenas said. "Yog-Sothoth has many doors, and some are strangely shaped."

"Is it possible the offerings were carried up on the lightning and the crystal vessel descended on it without shattering?"

"Unless it was some priest's trick," Martala said. "Priests in Egypt use all kinds of deceptions to insure the devotion of their worshippers."

"What are we to do now?" I asked her. "We've learned nothing concerning the fate of Alhazred."

"Follow me," she said in a grim tone. "I'm tired of creeping around like a mouse in a temple. If fate won't give us what we need to know, I will take it by force."

Chapter Nineteen

"**A**re you sure he's alone?" I asked Martala.

I removed my ear from the door. "I don't hear anyone else moving around in there."

"We should send Kanenas in to look around. He's so small and dark, the creature probably won't notice him in the dim light."

We crouched outside a doorway, where the insect-being we had followed down the broad corridors of the pyramid had vanished. It was the sleep time for the alien race, or so we guessed, since half the little spheres on the walls that provided the red glow for the interior had been turned off. Martala was determined to interrogate one of the monsters, but we could not risk sparking a general alarm.

Kanenas did not raise any objection to the plan. In the red murk of the corridor I could barely distinguish his outline against the black stones of the floor. The door had no locking mechanism. I slid it open silently a span or so, and the little man slipped through the crack. There was a minute of silence. Then a choked cry that sounded a bit like a cat coughing up a ball of hair, and the sound of something knocked over onto the floor.

"Let's go," Martala said.

We pushed the door aside and rushed through the opening. The reddish light was just as dull in the small chamber as it had been in the corridor, but by it I saw the insect creature holding Kanenas up in the grasp of its upper appendages. The little man made choking noises. One of the creature's hands, if such deformed things can be called hands, was around his throat.

I hit the monster over the head with the knob end of my bone dagger. It was a satisfying blow, and it staggered the thing, which allowed Kanenas to wriggle free of its grasp. I hit it again for good measure. This elicited a kind of whimpering whistle from its chest. Martala grabbed it by the neck and pulled it over backwards, then knelt on its body and showed it her dagger before pressing its blade to the thing's neck.

There were no other monsters in the room. I nodded for Anisah to close the door. The furniture was simple—a kind of table, a cabinet made of some polished wood, and a pad of furs on the floor, evidently intended for sleeping. On the table was a shrine that was composed of a small figurine of monstrous shape and a lamp that gave forth a reddish flame. The air was scented with some pungent spice that I guessed must emanate from the burning oil of the lamp.

"No noise," Martala hissed. "If you try to summon help, I will slit your throat."

The creature seemed to understand her intention. It nodded its misshapen head, its antennae dancing up and down.

"I will question, and you will answer. Do you understand the Greek language?"

Again it nodded.

This surprised me. Why should this alien creature understand Greek, I wondered? It seemed an unlikely stroke of good fortune.

"Where are you holding the necromancer Abdul Alhazred?"

A series of piping sounds, like discordant notes from a flute, came from an aperture in its thorax that opened and closed.

"I know your kind can speak our language," Martala said.

"I have heard you do so."

"How you know this?" it said in Greek. The accent was heavy but the words were clear enough. Its large eyes swiveled as it looked at each of us in turn.

"I destroyed the floating island your race placed in the sea on my world."

"You did this?" Its elongated body quivered, but whether with fear or anger I could not judge. "Stories are told in Great Nest of what you did."

"Your Great Nest means nothing to me."

"I was assigned to island. That is how I know your language. Just before I was to be sent there we receive news of its destruction. We thought it a malfunction in our energy source. We did not know your race destroyed it."

"Unless you want me to destroy your city, you will tell me what I wish to know."

It focused both its eyes upon her face. "This not our city."

"Whose city is it, then?"

"It belong to—" Here it made a sound that was like an ungreased wheel rolling along a steel rail.

"Not so loud. Do you mean the invisible giants?"

It nodded, causing the long antennae on its head to bob up and down.

"We call them the Old Ones," I said.

It turned its eyes to me. "Ancient they are beyond the years of your world."

"What do you know of Alhazred?" Martala asked.

"Those you call Old Ones give command to my race, bring him here, to accursed city."

"It was your people who sent the invisible demon that carried him up into the air?"

"No invisible demon. That was, what is your word, illusion."

"Why do you call this city accursed?" Anisah asked.

It clicked its mouthparts together from side to side. "Nest brothers hate city."

"Aren't you in partnership with the Old Ones?" I asked.

It shook its head vaguely and looked from me to Martala. It was evident that it did not understand.

"In accord with them. Their friends, their associates. Oath brothers."

"We are none of those things."

"What, then?"

It searched its mind for the right word. "Slaves. We slaves to Old Ones."

"Slaves? You mean all the members of your race in this world are enslaved to the Old Ones? Even your priest?"

The last word puzzled the creature.

"Your master of rituals."

It nodded vigorously. "Yes, all, even Chosen Elder of Appeasement."

Martala pushed against its thorax. "Where is Alhazred?" she demanded.

"Gone."

"Dead? Do you mean dead?"

"No, in suspended state. Alhazred not in this world."

"Do you mean he's not dead?" The Egyptian woman could not keep the anxious frustration from her voice.

"What you call death, no, not in that state."

The hand holding the dagger trembled. She blinked rapidly, and I saw a tear in the corner of her eye.

"Where is he?"

It spread its appendages and shook its head from side to side.

"No words for this place."

"I think it means there are no words in Greek to describe the place where he is being held," I said quickly to Martala before she decapitated the monster.

"Can you take us to this place?"

It hesitated, saying nothing.

"Can you show us the way there?"

"Yes, but it is dangerous place. Those who go there do not come back."

Kanenas had watched this exchange of words with the

monster in silence. "Is it accessed through a portal of Yog-Sothoth?"

"Yes, Yog-Sothoth, great lord of the Forever Nest whose eggs are always white." The antennae on the head of the thing trembled in awe.

"Show us the way to this portal, and I will release you unharmed," Martala said.

"Portal must be made," it said.

"Then make it."

"Only in the Great Hall can it be made."

"Can you make it? Answer with care. If you can make the portal, you have value to me."

"Yes, with aid of—" It searched for the word. "With aid of what you call mechanisms, I open it."

"These mechanisms, are they in the Great Hall?"

It nodded.

"Let us go there. You will work the mechanisms and open the portal. We will pass through it and leave you with your life. Agreed?"

"It will be so."

Martala allowed the thing to raise itself on its elongated lower limbs. We followed its awkward gait through empty, darkened corridors. It walked with its legs folded almost double, it's knees high in the air. Fortune favored us. No alert was sounded. It guided us back to the large chamber where we had watched the invisible Old One worshipped on its throne.

"Where are these mechanisms?" Martala asked.

It pointed at the two light projectors.

"Open the portal."

The insect-thing went to one of the machines and made it hum. Dazzling lights sprang forth from its mirrors and crystal lenses.

"Do not look directly at the lights," Martala ordered.

It positioned the beams of light, then crossed to the other machine and activated it. Similar lights began to dance from it.

"You must stand inside circle," it said, pointing at a pentacle that was inlaid in the black stones of the floor.

Hesitantly, we gathered together inside the bounds of the pentacle. I squinted through one eye at the humming, flashing machines and wondered if we were about to be turned into piles of smoking ash.

"For your knowledge, I possess the skill to throw this dagger with accuracy," Martala said.

"It is good to know," the creature said.

It went to each machine in turn and flipped some kind of switch. The lights became all the colors of the rainbow, and some colors that I had never seen. I felt myself becoming dizzy and staggered.

"Hold onto each other," Martala said. "Shut your eyes."

I first did as she ordered, then forced my eyes open to search for the monster. It stood between the machines, watching us. Was it my imagination, or did its posture exhibit satisfaction? I blinked and shut my eyes again. I heard it speak.

"None ever return."

Through my closed eyelids a blinding white light filled my head, and at the same time thunder crashed all around us.

Chapter Twenty

found myself floating, surrounded by an infinitude of bubbles of various sizes and hues. They were light and transparent, like the bubbles formed in froth or sea foam, but much larger—or I was much smaller. When I looked down to examine my body, I could not see it. Everything was moving bubbles, some rising, others falling, all bright with the colors of the peacock's tail. They seemed to glow with inner radiance, but when I studied them closely I found them empty inside.

"Hassid, is that you?" Anisah said.

Try as I might, I could not find her amid the foaming chaos.

"Sashi, what is going on?" I asked as panic closed my throat.

You have all been transformed by this strange world, she said in my mind, her beautiful human face floating in the air before me.

"Transformed in what way?"

You have become colored spheres of light.

It was a moment before I could comprehend her words. "Spheres? Do you mean these bubbles?"

That is what I mean.

"Anisah, I cannot see you. Where are you?" I said in a loud voice. But I discovered that I had no voice. The words echoed in my mind.

"I am before you, Hassid. Martala is here as well, and Kanenas."

"I can see no one. My view is obscured by a kind of greasy froth of bubbles."

"We are within it as well," Anisah said. "I feel myself to be greatly changed."

Where is she, Sashi? I thought.

Anisah is before you. The sphere that is colored violet is her form.

I looked, or seemed to look, for even the act of looking felt strange and unnatural, and before me I discerned a floating sphere that rose and fell gently on the air. It was a delicate hue of violet. The light of some unseen sun shone through its sides and made it glisten. It was quite beautiful, but my fear was too great to allow me to appreciate its beauty.

"Where is Martala?" I asked aloud.

The golden sphere.

"And Kanenas?"

The small sphere that is colored like a bright ruby.

These other bubbles floated at varying distances from me amid a mass of spheres that circulated on invisible and unfelt currents. I could see nothing beyond this chaos of color and movement. In a hesitant voice, I told the others what Sashi had said to me. I seemed to speak, but knew no words came from my lips, for I had no lips.

"What color did she say I was?" Martala asked.

"Golden."

"I see you, Hassid. You are a beautiful spring green," Anisah said.

"The colors must express aspects of our natures," Kanenas said. "What am I?"

"Bright red."

"That is of the fire," he said with satisfaction. "As it should be."

"What are we to do, Martala?" I asked. "We cannot progress. We have no direction, nothing to guide us, no legs with which to walk. I see nothing around us but an endless ocean of froth that seethes and roils."

"You abandon hope too easily, Hassid," she said in my mind. "Let us try to move together in a single direction. Use the force of your will. I will go ahead. The rest of you, follow me if you can."

Her golden bubble began to slowly drift between those that rose and fell around her. I willed myself to go after her, and to my surprise I closed the distance that had opened between us. On either side I perceived in some way that Kanenas and Anisah were moving with me.

"Now we need to know which way to go," Martala said.

"I have an idea," Anisah said. "We should all concentrate on Alhazred, and desire to move toward him."

"It's at least worth a try," Martala said.

"I have never met the man," Kanenas reminded her.

"Then you must concentrate on your memory of me."

Conjuring up the image of my teacher in my mind as I remembered him, I concentrated on the memory of his voice and the manner of his movements. After a short while we all began to drift in the same direction, but whether up, down, or to the side, I could not tell. There was no fixed point of reference. Everything moved around us, and we moved through it, but in unison, almost as though a singular breeze were blowing that affected us alone.

This continued for what seemed to me a very long time—hours at least, perhaps days. The light did not change. The mass of colored spheres that floated around us was ever-changing, but uniform in its variety. I had no sense of motion other than by marking the locations of the spheres that drifted past us. It became an effort to keep the image of Alhazred's features in my mind. I reached a point where I could not remember them at all, and concentrated only on the memory of the sound of his voice and his manner of speaking. We ceased to talk between ourselves. What was there to say while drifting in this endless, chaotic sea of trembling colored spheres?

"I perceive something ahead," Martala said.

I cast my sense of sight forward, through the curtain of bubbles that veiled it. It was a kind of pattern or structure that was stationary. Once seen, it stood out with remarkable vividness against the formless, moving background. I distinguished a cluster of colorless spheres arranged geometrically. There were twelve of them. They surrounded a thirteenth sphere and enfolded it at their center, pressing in upon it. This central sphere glistened and flashed with all the colors of the rainbow. It was so bright and beautiful, I found it difficult to hold my mind upon it, in the same way it is hard to stare upward at the sun.

The golden bubble that was Martala rushed forward.

"Alhazred," she said. Just that, but in that single word there was a volume of meaning—love, longing, regret, concern, anger, hope, and fear but not for herself.

There was no response from the rainbow bubble in the center of the cluster, which I took to be some kind of prison.

"Why doesn't he answer?" Anisah asked.

"He is cut off by the spheres that surround him," I said with sudden intuition. "He may not even perceive us."

"We must set him free."

"How? When I started on this quest I had a sword and a dagger. Now I don't even have arms or legs."

"Your mind is your weapon," Kanenas said.

"In what way do you mean?"

"What you will to be, strongly enough, comes to pass in this world."

"Kanenas is right," Martala said. "Hassid, imagine that you have your sword in your hand. Use it to cut through this cage of bubbles."

With a doubtful mind, I tried to imagine as clearly as possible that I had a right arm, and that in my right hand was the hilt of my sword. I visualized in my mind cutting and slashing with its blade at the twelve spheres than enclosed the thirteenth. Martala moved closer to the enclosure. I saw nothing but she must have been imagining herself wielding her tiny dagger. One of the bubbles near her golden sphere burst and vanished, then another. The sphere that I slashed with my imagined sword suddenly popped to nothingness.

I felt a heaviness fall over my mind. It felt like having a woolen cloak pressed over my face. I fought to cast it off, but it seemed to stifle me in some way and to obscure my senses.

"They are fighting back. Strike harder, Hassid." Martala's voice was clear but faint, as though I were hearing it over a great distance of space.

I redoubled my efforts, slashing and thrusting at the barrier of spheres. Another burst, than another. They began to break apart and separate from the rainbow sphere at their center. Soon there were only three remaining. They rose and floated away from us.

"Do not pursue them," Martala said. "See to Alhazred."

This was easier spoken than done. The rainbow sphere floated before us, the colors coming and going across its transparent surface like reflections of sunlight. The four of us clustered around it.

"Alhazred, can you hear me?" Martala spoke, or seemed to speak in my mind.

There was no answer.

"Maybe he's dead," Kanenas said.

"No, look at the colors," Anisah said. "Those are his thoughts. I believe he is dreaming."

"How am I to wake him?" There was a plaintive note in Martala's question.

"Are we even sure it is him?" I said.

"It must be Alhazred. We were drawn directly to him."

It is Alhazred, Sashi said in my mind. *I sense his presence.*

We watched and waited in silence. I hardly dared to hope.

A new voice came in my mind. "Where are we?"

"Alhazred," Martala said with joy. "It is you."

"If you are Martala, you have greatly changed."

"It's this accursed world. It transformed us all, even you."

"My memory is returning to me. I was taken from the marketplace in Damascus."

"And torn to pieces," I said. "Or so it appeared."

"So that is how he contrived my death."

"He? Do you have an enemy?" Kanenas asked.

"I do not recognize you," Alhazred told him.

"This is Kanenas, a homunculus," I explained. "He opened a portal that took us from the Soumela Monastery to the house of the Shenghuo Sect on the Plateau of Leng."

"But this is not Leng."

"No. We passed from Leng to a strange world with a city of giants, and from that city to this place. We do not know where we are."

"I have some idea. Thank you for coming to rescue me, Hassid. It was brave of you."

"It was the least I could do for my esteemed teacher."

"But who is this? Can it be Anisah? I sense her presence."

"I am here, Alhazred," she said. "In spirit, if not in body."

"How are we to escape from this place?" Martala demanded. "That is all that matters."

"I did not come all this way just to escape," Alhazred said.

"You didn't come at all. You were abducted," I reminded him.

"True, but it was not done entirely without forethought. I could not know how I would be taken, or when, or by what route, but I had reason to believe that my enemy preferred to torture rather than kill me. I knew what my ultimate destination would be, and here I am. Now I must accomplish the task for which I came."

Chapter Twenty-One

"What is this task, that was so important you risked your life to accomplish it?" Martala demanded.

"I came here to procure the elixir of Yog-Sothoth."

"We don't even know where *here* is."

"I thought that was obvious. We are inside the body of Yog-Sothoth itself."

"Inside a god," I said wonderingly. "Can such a thing be?"

"Remember the descriptions you have read of Yog-Sothoth, young Hassid. How do they speak of him?"

I cast my mind back to my necromantic studies. "They refer to a kind of foam that is composed of colored globules that are like the bubbles that rise in water when a swimmer exhales."

"Even so. Could there be a better description of the world around us?"

On every side colored bubbles rose and fell, bumping gently into each other as they passed. I saw that he was correct.

"What can we do in these ridiculous bodies?" Kanenas demanded. "We have no arms or legs."

"This world is shaped by the power of mind. It was your will that drew you to me, your will that shattered my prison. I believe that if we concentrate with a great enough force on our bodies of flesh, they will be returned to us."

"It is at least worth trying," Martala said.

I tried to repress my skepticism and thought of my physical body.

"Close your eyes, everyone," Alhazred said. "We have no eyes, but imagine doing it. Hassid, don't forget to remember your sword."

With my eyes shut, it was easy to imagine my body. I could feel my arms and legs. I moved my fingers experimentally. There was a strange scent in the air. I thought that I could feel solid stone under my boots.

"Open your eyes."

I did as he ordered, and was astonished to find that the floating bubbles had been replaced by a chamber in a building of stone blocks that was illuminated by torchlight. Nine warriors lay dead on the floor around us in pools of their own blood, fatal wounds evident on their bodies.

Feeling at my waist, I fingered the hilts of my sword and dagger where they hung from my belt. I stomped my foot, and felt the hardness of the flags under my boot as the sound echoed from the high ceiling. The chamber was empty. There was no furniture, no carpet, no tapestries covering the walls. The space had a dead feel to it, as though it had never been a dwelling for living things.

Turning, I saw that the others had regained their bodies and clothing. But I was not prepared for the sight of Kanenas. The little black man with his oversized head had vanished. In his place stood a handsome youth of normal dimensions who had blue eyes and curling golden hair. He looked like a young Alexander. He was completely naked, and his male organ stood up against his muscular abdomen.

Anisah blushed a deep rose tint in her cheeks and turned her face away.

"Baast preserve us," Martala muttered. "It was bad enough before." She took off her head covering and passed it to Kanenas. "Tie this around your waist."

"How is it you are so changed?" I asked as he was concealing his virility under the headscarf.

"I always wanted to have a body like the rest of you," he said with a faint smile. "It must have been hidden in my thoughts when I willed myself to return to the flesh."

Alhazred also was very different from my memory of him. In Damascus when he had presided over my lessons in necromancy he had appeared to be an elderly man, but he stood here before me in the body of a man no older than myself. The gray had left his hair, and the wrinkles around his mouth and jade eyes had vanished away. He wore a black Persian tunic trimmed with silver threads.

"What are you staring at, Hassid?" he asked me.

"You are greatly changed from when I last looked upon you, Alhazred."

He laughed. "You see me as I would like to see myself. I regard my deformities as a mask, and this unblemished face as my own. Also, I have no need to pretend to be burdened by my years, as I did in Damascus."

"To me you always look the same," Martala said, staring at him with loving eyes.

"We must hurry," Alhazred told her. "The slaying of my guards will have alerted things within this castle of the mind that possess greater power, and will prove much more difficult to kill."

"Where are we going?" she asked.

"Up."

"Why up?"

"All aspiration leads upward. I aspire to attain the elixir of Yog-Sothoth, so it must be above us, probably in the room of a tower."

Anisah, Kanenas and I trotted after them as they exchanged this banter.

"We always seem to be climbing," Kanenas said with a note of exasperation in his new voice.

"Be glad we're not falling," I muttered.

Now that Alhazred was here, Martala seemed to have forgotten our existence. The two of them moved together as a single being joined at the head and the heart. She had attained what she most desired. Alhazred was alive, and she was with him. How could we three be of any importance to her? I felt irritation at being so quickly and easily displaced from her thoughts, like a tool she had used, then cast aside when it was no longer needed.

The two ahead of us found a set of stairs and ran up them two steps at a time. We followed at their heels. I scarcely saw the rooms we passed through as we climbed staircase after staircase. Strangely, I did not feel tired. It occurred to me that since my body was only a seeming thing in this world, there was no reason to be fatigued. We were probably floating upward as colored bubbles. I felt my sense of reality waver, and quickly put this capricious thought from my mind. Instead, I concentrated on making myself believe that the stone walls around us were solid and real.

At length we reached a spiral staircase and ascended its narrow stone steps more slowly in a single file. The light was dim and the worn edges of the stones treacherous beneath our boots. From some distant part of the castle I heard a kind of shriek such as might issue from the beak of a giant bird. It was an ominous sound.

"We are drawing near to what you seek, Alhazred," Anisah said. "I can feel it."

He paused to glance over his shoulder at her.

"Trust what she says," Martala told him. She described the way Anisah's prescience had served us.

"Your father is a great seer and your mother a queen of the fey," he said to the girl. "I'm not surprised you possess the gift of sight."

"It's more a feeling than vision," she said.

We climbed a short while more, and emerged onto a balcony at the top of a stone tower. An arch extended from it, supporting a narrow bridge without railings that led across space to another tower with a conical roof of slates. At the point of this roof rose a flagpole from which fluttered a black flag. Upon the flag was the face of a grinning white skull, and above and below it, the horseshoe-shaped astrological symbols of the Head and Tail of the Dragon. The Abbot Nicodemus had worn them on his medallion. From my studies I know that these symbols represented the going in and coming out from the portals of Yog-Sothoth. I peered nervously over the edge of the balcony and searched all around, but saw nothing except a whiteness that was like a thin mist. The bases of the two towers disappeared down into it.

"We must cross this bridge," Alhazred said.

"That won't be difficult," Martala said. "It's narrow, but it looks solid enough to support our weight."

She started forward. As she stepped onto the bridge, the wooden door in the opposite tower opened, and a warrior stepped out who was covered from head to toe in armor. He wore a cuirass upon his breast that shone like polished gold, and over his head a silver helmet that completely concealed his face. Every part of his body was protected by glittering steel. In his gauntlets he grasped the hilt of a great sword, the straight blade of which was taller than a man standing. He supported this sword vertically before him, leaning its blade neither to the left nor to the right.

Alhazred drew Martala gently back by the shoulder and stepped in front of her onto the bridge.

"I seek my heart's desire," he said in a curiously formal tone.

"It is not lawful that you be given it," the shining warrior answered in clear Greek.

"Then I must steal it."

"I am the Guardian of the Gate. None obtain their heart's desire except through me."

I wondered to hear this stilted and artificial exchange of words between them. They sounded like actors on a stage, speaking parts they had rehearsed.

"What must I do to cross the threshold?" Alhazred asked.

"I will pose three riddles, which you must answer rightly before I will permit you to pass."

"And if I fail?"

"You die, and your companions with you."

"Is all this no more than a game to you?"

"All of life is a game you mortals play . . . until you lose."

"Is there never a way to win?"

"Only one, as you well know."

"Pose your first riddle. We will solve it."

The guardian did not dispute Alhazred's inclusion of the rest of us in the contest, from which I inferred that we would be allowed to confer regarding the solutions to the riddles. This did not cheer me. I have never been good with riddles. From somewhere below me within the depths of the tower I heard another shriek, this time louder than before. Whatever made the heart-chilling sound was coming closer.

Chapter Twenty-Two

"Shall we begin?" the Guardian asked.

Alhazred nodded.

"What is that which has been tomorrow, and will be yesterday?"

"That is your first riddle?"

"It is."

"It's very brief."

"Do you have an answer? You may confer among yourselves."

Alhazred turned and approached us.

"Yesterday, tomorrow—It's some kind of time riddle."

"Has been tomorrow, what does that mean?" Kanenas said. "How can something be in the past tomorrow?"

"I should mention to you all that I will limit the time you take to answer. Discuss the riddle but do not be too long about it," the Guardian said.

I looked at him, and saw something slide behind his left leg. It was sinuous and gray, like the body of a serpent.

"Did you see that?" I asked Anisah.

"I saw nothing. What did you see, Hassid?"

"I'm not sure. In this place we cannot trust our eyes. Maybe it was nothing."

"We have the answer," Alhazred said, raising his head from his muttered conversation with Martala.

"Are you sure? Think carefully before you speak. If the

answer you give is wrong, you will all surely die."

"Today," Alhazred said without hesitation. The present day was once tomorrow, and in time it will become yesterday."

"Correct," the guardian said without emotion. "You have solved the first riddle."

"Then ask the second," Alhazred said.

"Without me day would be as night, and night be equal to the day."

"Is that the riddle?"

"It is. Give your answer."

"In a moment or two. I must confer with my companions." He stepped back to where we stood together. "What do you think, Martala?"

"My mind is empty," she said.

"It has to do with light and darkness," I said. "Day and night are mentioned. What do you think, Kanenas?"

"Why ask me?" Kanenas grumbled. "I have no skill with riddles."

"I think I know," Anisah said in a quiet voice.

I looked at the Guardian. He seemed indifferent to our talk, if indeed his ears were keen enough to hear us. There was a curious bristling on his shining armor. I blinked and looked harder, but now it was gone. For a moment I thought his armor to be covered with hair. While I stared, Alhazred stepped two paces toward him.

"The answer to the second riddle is the eye," he said. "For without the eye, day and night are the same."

"Correct," the Guardian said. "Either you or your companions are uncommonly clever. So much so that I am sure you will have no difficulty with the third riddle."

"Then ask it."

"I am an assistant to those who write, a friend to the serious, an enemy to the giddy and dissipated. I am courted by all who love wisdom, and despised only by fools. What am I?"

"We shall confer and give you our answer," Alhazred said, and walked back to us.

"A pen?" Martala said uncertainly.

"Do those who love wisdom court a pen?" Alhazred asked.

"They may, if they want to write."

"How is a pen an enemy to the giddy and dissipated?" I asked.

"A book, then," she said.

"Again I ask, how is a book an enemy to the giddy?"

"I don't know," she admitted. "But it must be something to do with scholarship."

"I'm waiting," the Guardian said.

I looked at him. Tentacles were sliding slowly out of the eye slot in his helmet visor and wriggling like gray worms before his face. Larger ones crept around his body from his back and waved in the air. As I watched, they multiplied.

"You must see this," I said to Anisah.

She looked long at the guardian. "I see nothing changed. Perhaps if you tell me what you are looking at, I may begin to see it."

I described the moving tentacles that had by now enfolded the guardian in a writhing mass that completely obscured his human shape. She still could not see them. Kanenas, who had listened, admitted that he saw no change.

"Either I am going mad, or this armored warrior is not quite what he seems to be," I told them. "I must warn Alhazred."

My teacher had already stepped forward again to confront the Guardian of the Threshold.

"The answer to the third riddle is contemplation."

"Incorrect," the Guardian said.

"I don't believe you. It must be the right answer. Contemplation assists those who compose writings, it comforts those of serious mind, it limits giddiness and drunkenness, is sought by those who are scholars, and despised by fools. How is it not the answer?"

"The correct answer is thought."

"But contemplation is a type of thinking," Alhazred objected.

"Your answer to the third riddle is incorrect. I shall now kill you all."

Instead of answering, Alhazred rushed forward, drew his sword, and plunged it into the breast of the Guardian. The blade passed through the shining armor, which I could dimly see beneath the mass of writhing tentacles that covered it. The Guardian staggered back and dropped his great sword.

Reaching forward with both hands to grasp the wounded warrior's helmet, Alhazred threw himself backward and down onto the stone bridge, drawing the Guardian after him. It was a perilous move that brought Alhazred to the very edge of the bridge, but the weight of the Guardian, if I may so call the ball of snakes he had become, was too great to be halted in its motion, and he tumbled across the necromancer and over the side. I peered over the edge. He slowly fading to nothingness as the mist closed around his monstrous falling form.

"It was not in his mind to let us pass, no matter what answer we gave for the third riddle," Anisah said. "I sensed his malign intention."

"Did none of you see that he was a mass of entwined gray worms?" I asked in frustration.

Alhazred looked at Martala, who shook her head, then at Anisah, who lowered her gaze.

"I know what I saw," I said.

"I don't doubt you, Hassid. In this place, our minds craft our perception. You saw what was real to you, as we all did."

The harsh scream I had heard before echoed through the mist. It was impossible to tell where it originated. The sound seemed to come from all around us.

"Please tell me you heard that," I said.

"We heard it," Martala said.

"We must hurry, we haven't much time," Alhazred said. "I fear the one who watches over this world has become aware of my purpose and is seeking us out the way a wolf follows the scent of its quarry."

"Do you speak of Yog-Sothoth?" Martala asked as we hurried across the bridge.

"Not Yog-Sothoth, but the one who dwells within the portals of Yog-Sothoth."

"Within the portals? Do you mean within this castle?"

"No, Hassid, I mean within the very portals themselves. It dwells in the interstices between worlds, between the here and the there, between the past and the future."

"I have never heard of such a being," Kanenas said.

"Few have. Its existence is only hinted at in a few rare texts. They refer to it as the Dweller Beyond the Threshold."

The door of the second tower was shut. It appeared to be a simple door of vertical planks of what looked like oak, bound together with black iron straps that extended across its full width. Alhazred paused before it, then carefully reached for the latch. It came up easily and the door swung inward. Inside, light glowed with a kind of greenish hue. I entered cautiously with my hand around the hilt of my sword.

The chamber was round like the tower itself, and bare save for a pedestal in its center that appeared to be made of polished black glass. Upon the pedestal rested a large emerald that cast forth a glow strong enough to illuminate the entire space.

"Is that the thing you came for?" Martala asked.

"It must be—it can be nothing else."

"Then take it."

An ear-splitting shriek from outside shook the tower under our feet. The sound was filled with rage. I went to the open doorway and looked out. The bridge was gone along with the first tower by which we had ascended. There was only the featureless white mist.

"The mist has ascended around us. I see nothing else."

A shadow loomed out of the mist as I spoke these words. It was like the wall of a building that approached with frightening speed. As it drew near the tower, I saw that it was a kind of grotesque face. It continued to come nearer. I stepped back into the chamber. A single staring eye of cyclopean size filled the opening of the doorway and rolled this way and that, peering in at us. Summoning what little courage remained in my heart, I darted forward and slammed the door. Its inner latch clicked into place.

"What did you see?" Martala demanded.

I described the face in the mist. As I spoke, the tower was shaken with another shriek of fury.

"Was it a human face?" Alhazred asked. He did not seem troubled by the cry of the monster. I wondered that he could remain so composed.

I tried to remember what the face looked like, but found that for some reason I was unable. "I can't quite call it back in my mind. I don't think it was human."

"Your mind struggled to give the thing you saw a form that would be comprehensible to you," he said. "Now it purges the image from your memory to keep you from going mad, in the same way it purges your nightmares when you awake from sleep."

Again the howling scream shook the tower.

"Can it get in?" Kanenas demanded. He stood trembling with fear.

"I do not believe so," Alhazred told him. "If it could do so, we would already be dead."

"Perhaps we are dead, and this is a nightmare of the afterlife," Anisah said.

"Don't say that," Martala told her. "Remember, thoughts become real in this place."

"Maybe we can think it to death," Kanenas suggested.

"It doesn't work that way," Alhazred said as he approached the great emerald and studied it without touching it. "Our thoughts provide forms that our minds can cope with, that is all."

"You struck the Guardian of the Gate with your sword," I reminded him.

"I struck it with something that would not have killed it, which is why I had to throw it off the bridge."

The golden-haired youth who had once been the misshapen homunculus paced around the chamber, pressing his hands against its stone wall.

"How are we to get out of this place? There is only one entrance, and if we step outside into the mist, that shrieking monster will surely slay us."

As if to provide affirmation, another shriek shook the tower.

"What exactly is that thing outside?" Martala demanded.

Alhazred straightened away from the jewel he had been closely studying and smiled at her.

"I became aware of its existence while carrying out my research. It became aware of me at the same time. We played a dangerous game. I continued my studies, but turned my mind away from it. I could not speak to you about it, or even think of it in a direct way, without drawing it to our house. As it began to suspect my intention, an abductor was sent to capture me."

"Why not an assassin?" she asked.

"That I cannot say for certain, but I believe it wanted to interrogate me to find out if I had communicated my knowledge to any others about the location of the prize I sought." His expression darkened. "Although there may be another reason. My sprites forced open many gates of Yog-Sothoth. I sensed outrage from it, as though I had violated something sacred."

"It will never let us leave this tower," she said. "It wants our knowledge of this place and its existence to die with us."

Chapter Twenty-Three

How long we waited, I had no way to reckon the hours, but it seemed an eternity. The giant god or devil outside did not leave. Periodically we heard its cries, and felt them in our bones as they rattled the tower. We sat on the wooden floor of the jewel chamber, except for Kanenas, who continued to pace restlessly. As yet Alhazred had not touched the jewel. The sense gathered in my heart that he delayed touching it because he knew that when he did so, bad things would happen.

"We will die of hunger and thirst," Martala said after a long silence.

"Do you feel hungry?" Alhazred asked her.

"Now that you speak of it, no."

"Time moves at a different pace in this world. In all the days you say have elapsed since my capture, I have not eaten. Yet I feel no hunger."

"Even so, if we stay here long enough we will die of thirst." she reasoned.

"How can we get out?" I said. "Even if we could evade that giant god that waits outside, there is nothing but mist. It will not support us."

"We are bubbles, remember? We will float," Alhazred said with a smile.

"I fear that monster will grab us in its claws and we will pop," Kanenas said.

"Perhaps if one of us went outside, as a sacrifice, the monster would be satisfied and go away," Anisah said.

This was an odd thing for the girl to say. I looked at her narrowly, but her serene face did not display any loss of composure.

"That is doubtful," Alhazred told her. "The Dweller hates me for my violations of Yog-Sothoth's gateways and wants my soul to torment for eternity."

"What if we sent you out alone?" Kanenas stopped his pacing and turned to confront the necromancer. "Would it go away and leave the rest of us?"

"I am not disposed to try your plan, homunculus."

"What if we gave you no choice?" the golden-haired youth said with a smile.

"Speak like that again and I will cut your throat," Martala told Kanenas. "Alhazred's sword may be imaginary, but my dagger is real."

"But my throat is not real," he said with a chuckle. "You would be cutting the air two cubits above my head."

"Or popping your bubble," I said. "Do not try her patience, little man."

"Don't you want to get out of this place alive, Hassid?" he demanded.

"We leave together or not at all," Martala's tone allowed no argument.

Again we fell silent, and Kanenas resumed his pacing, which was beginning to annoy me.

Martala looked into Alhazred's eyes in the green glow from the jewel. "I assume you have a plan to get out of this place."

"Not a plan, exactly. I would not call it a plan."

"What would you call it?"

"A slender hope, but better than no hope."

"What are we waiting for? Use it," Kanenas said.

"Patience, little man. I have been reconstructing in my mind a symbol that I saw many years ago, long before you were spawned in an alchemical vessel, before even young

Hassid here was a gleam in his father's lusty eye."

"How long will it take you to remember it?"

"It is done." Alhazred stood up and stretched his back with his arms over his head.

The rest of us stood. We had sat on the floor for what seemed an age. In spite of the lack of a fire, I did not feel cold, or stiff for that matter. I wondered if Alhazred's stretch had been only a nervous gesture.

"Move aside," he told us.

We separated ourselves at a distance from where he stood. Kanenas stopped pacing and stood behind me, watching over my shoulder.

Alhazred faced the blank stone wall. Extending his right hand, he traced a complex symbol on the air in front of him. Its lines glowed in red fire and sustained themselves on the air after he finished. In outline it had the shape of two squares rotated one over the other to form a star of eight points. A strange symbol filled its center. He raised his arms above his head with his fingers opened wide and spoke in a resonant tone.

"Great goddess, I summon you by your true name, which you yourself confided to me after I set you free from your bondage of death. You told me that should I ever want your aid, I need only speak your name and you would surely come. This I now do, mighty goddess. I call upon you and summon you, Ho-sien-ku."

The glowing symbol burst into flame and exploded in all directions. In its place stood a slender woman in a long gown of cloth-of-gold that was covered in seed pearls. This tight and revealing garment extended from a collar around her slender neck to the beaded slippers on her feet. Her black hair fell in a glossy cascade over the front of her right shoulder. Rouge gave color to her ivory cheeks. The lips of her small mouth, reddened with henna, resembled the petals of a rose. Kohl lined her dark eyes, accentuating their size and mystery. Her facial features were similar to those of the Shenghuo brothers. They told me she was originally from the land of Chen. Looking down the length of her body, I realized that she was not standing on the floor, but floated just above it. Her entire outline glowed with its own pearl-white radiance.

"Why have you called me here?" she asked Alhazred in a mild tone. The language was strange in my ears, but somehow I could understand its meaning.

"I remind you of your pledge to me, Ho-sien-ku. When I liberated you from your prison of mummified flesh, you swore to come to my aid if I was ever in need. My companions and I need your help."

She looked around the chamber. He eyes came to rest on the shining green jewel on its black pedestal.

"You play a dangerous game, Alhazred."

"Will you help us to escape from this place?"

Outside the wall of the tower, the Dweller Beyond the Threshold howled and shrieked, and the entire tower shook as though blasted by a storm wind.

"What is it you wish of me?"

"Carry us back to my house in Damascus."

"That I cannot do," she said. "It is beyond my power. I can carry you and your companions no further than the realm you occupied prior to your ascent to this world."

"If that is all you can do, it must suffice."

"I have one condition."

"What is that?"

She pointed at the pedestal. "You cannot carry away the jewel with you. It would be a violation of the very stuff and fabric of reality. It is a thing forbidden by the laws of Yog-Sothoth."

Alhazred gazed at the jewel, which was almost near enough for him to reach out and touch. "Is there no way it could be done?"

"It would demand a price that I do not believe you wish to pay."

"What kind of price?"

"A sacrifice."

He glanced at me, then looked for a longer moment at Martala. "I would be willing to pay the price."

"Not you, Alhazred," the goddess said. She pointed at Anisah. "This one."

"Why not me? I'm the reason they are here."

"She has power that you do not possess, power you cannot even imagine."

"Alhazred, why are you talking about sacrifice?" Martala said. "I don't want the emerald, I want you with me."

"I can only offer myself. I cannot speak for the lives of my companions."

"Your life is not enough, necromancer."

His gaze wandered back to the jewel, then to Anisah, who watched and listened in silence. I saw her nod her head almost imperceptibly.

"Forget the damn jewel," Martala said, anger in her voice. "It's not worth your life, or Anisah's, or anyone else's."

"I very much concur," Kanenas said.

"You do not understand its power," Alhazred told her gently.

"What is it? The stone of alchemy? Do you plan to pave Damascus with gold? We have enough gold already; we need no more of it."

"Shall I carry you and your companions back to the world you left before coming to this one?" the goddess asked.

Alhazred stared at Anisah. There was concentration in his eyes, and concern. Her face was calm and her gaze serene. At that moment she was even more beautiful than the shining goddess.

"Carry us back," Alhazred said.

The goddess raised her arm and waved her hand through the air in a gesture that seemed almost negligent. It began to stir and swirl around us, rising in the span of a few heartbeats from a whisper to a roar. The walls of the chamber dimmed around me. I saw Martala shout at Alhazred, but could not hear what she said. Above the roar of the wind the enraged shriek of the monstrous god outside sounded.

My sight dimmed and I felt a dizziness that staggered me. Just before blackness closed over my sight, I saw Alhazred reach back with his left hand and snatch the emerald from its mounting on the pedestal.

Chapter Twenty-four

Stumbling forward, I caught myself before I fell to my knees and looked around in confusion. At first I thought it was night. Then I remembered that the dull red glow was what passed for daylight in the city of the Old Ones.

I looked up and saw the sooty ember of the sun between the looming monolithic buildings that towered on either side. It was barely brighter than the black sky around it. The stars cast more light. Alhazred stood beside me, supporting Martala by one of her arms as she swayed and nearly fell. She blinked and shook her head to clear it.

Something groaned in a childlike voice. I saw Kanenas a short distance away, once more in his small black body. He picked himself up from the paving stones of the street and stood swaying, rubbing his head. Martala's headscarf had fallen from his shrunken hips. I picked it up, untied the knot in it, and gave it back to Martala, who accepted it absently.

"Where is Anisah?" she said, glancing around. Her voice rose in alarm. "Where is Anisah?"

Alhazred said nothing.

She peered through the dim light, looking for the girl, then began to call her name.

"That may not be wise," Kanenas said. "We don't want to attract the attention of the giants."

"Who are these giants?" Alhazred asked.

"Didn't you encounter them when they brought you here?"

"I must have been unconscious. I don't remember this place."

"They are invisible. They kill with bolts of lightning. The humans who dwell like rats in this city call them the Old Ones."

Martala returned. Her hands were balled into fists. She stood close to Alhazred and glared up at him. Her fury was potent enough to cause him to take a half step backward.

"You took it, didn't you?"

"Yes, I took it," he said quietly.

"Anisah is gone. You took the jewel and now Anisah is gone. Do you know what that means?"

"I know very well what it means," he said. There was a weight in his voice.

"You sacrificed that innocent child for a jewel?"

"She sacrificed herself."

"What?"

"She indicated that she wished to sacrifice herself."

"Indicated? How? She said nothing."

"It was in her gaze. She nodded her head."

Martala stared at him, laughed shortly, then looked away. When she looked back her dagger was in her hand. Alhazred made no motion to defend himself. I do not believe he ever came nearer to death than at that moment. I did not dare to move or even to breathe. Her slender body trembled with fury. Then she turned away, and when she turned back the knife was no longer in her hand.

"What you did is something for which I can never forgive you," she said.

He said nothing, but turned his face away. His eyes fell on me. I stood staring at him.

"What?" he barked in irritation.

"Your face."

He grunted in comprehension. "What you see is my true face, Hassid. This is how I look when I forget to renew the glamour that improves my appearance."

It was horrifying. Where his nose should have been there was only a dark cavity, and his cheeks were deeply scarred. He had no ears. He muttered a few words in a language I did not understand and made a gesture with his hand in front of his face. Suddenly he was a handsome man once again. It was the way he had appeared in the bubble world, after we assumed our human shapes.

Kanenas waddled several steps away and stood with his grotesque little head tilted to one side. He cupped his hand behind one of his large ears and seemed to listen. I heard him sniff the air.

"A giant is coming," he hissed. "We need to run. Now."

"Where is it?" Alhazred asked.

Kanenas pointed up the street. I looked and saw nothing, but I felt a kind of presence. The air swirled. A blinding bolt of lightning lanced toward us, striking the black stones of the road next to Alhazred.

"Run," he cried.

The command was unnecessary. I was already in flight before he spoke it. Kanenas ran in front of me and in spite of his short legs, widened the distance. For such a tiny creature, he moved with astonishing quickness. We ran away from the invisible presence that made the air crackle around it as it prepared to strike a second time. Another bolt flashed out as we were turning a corner into a side street, but this also missed. We continued to run for several minutes before stopping to catch our breath. The strange air of this world burned my lungs and made me gasp. I smelled the lightning.

"Whatever powers it has, it does not move very quickly," Alhazred said.

"How are we going to get out of this world?" I asked.

"If we were on our own world, and I had enough time, I could open a portal for us to escape," Kanenas said.

"Can't you take us back to Damascus? Or even back to the Plateau of Leng?"

He shook his head.

"Where is the portal that brought you into this world? Can you find it?" Alhazred asked.

"It was a well. I think it lies ahead of us," Martala said, not looking at Alhazred. "This way."

We hurried after her. The street opened into a broad empty space. I recognized it as the plaza where we had entered this world, and saw the low wall of the well projecting above the paving stones. We ran toward it, and I peered into its opening. At the level of the plaza there was a solid floor of material that resembled black glass. With care, I swung my leg over the rim of the well and stood up on it.

"It's no use, Alhazred," I said. "The well sealed itself behind us."

"Can we break through it?"

I jumped up and down on the surface. It was as hard as granite.

"With what? We have no hammers."

"It probably doesn't matter. It's a magic thing—it was made not to be broken."

Something cracked softly at the edge of the plaza. A breeze stirred my hair. I looked but saw nothing.

"I think the giant is coming toward us," I said.

Alhazred ignored me. He knelt on one knee before Kanenas.

"You say you cannot open a portal between worlds. Can you open a portal here, in this world?"

"Perhaps," the little man said, "but I would need to be familiar with the place where it opened, and I know nothing of this world but bits of this endless city of night."

"You know the well, and you know how it looked as you were ascending it."

Kanenas's eyes widened. "It might work. If the top of the tower extends into this world, it might work."

"Try it. We don't have much time."

The plaza was broad, and the invisible creature advancing toward us moved slowly, but there was little time before another bolt of lightning lanced out from it. *We should be running,* I thought, but I held my tongue against my teeth.

The little man stood on the top of the wall around the well and began to make gestures in the air that were similar to the gestures I had seen him making in the Soumela Monastery. He muttered to himself.

"Haste is indicated," I said, trying to keep my voice steady.

"Unless you stop talking, we will all die," Kanenas said.

"Spread yourself around the plaza," Alhazred ordered. "Try to distract it away from the well."

We ran in three directions while the little man continued to mutter and wave his hands in the air. I saw that Alhazred had chosen to run toward the crackling sound.

"This way, monster," he shouted.

The crackling paused. There was silence. A moment later a bolt of lightning darted in his direction. He anticipated the attack and leapt to the side barely in time.

"Help Alhazred," Martala shouted to me. She ran forward, waving her arms.

"Over here," I yelled, approaching the invisible monster from the other side.

The crackling died away. All three of us jumped at the same moment, since we had no way of knowing in which direction the lightning would be thrown. It was toward Martala, who was barely quick enough.

"Your headscarf is on fire," I yelled to her.

She tore it off and cast it away from her without a glance. It continued to burn on the paving stones.

Another bolt flashed forth, seemingly from the empty air. The sulfurous smell of the lightning was strong. I forgot to leap aside in my concern for Martala. Fortunately for me, the weapon was directed at Alhazred, who only just managed to avoid it with an anticipatory twist of his body.

The thin, childlike voice of the homunculus sounded above the low crackle, which was gathering its strength for another bolt. "It's open. Be quick, I don't know how long I can hold it."

159

This is when the danger is greatest, I thought. We all converged on the well, which made us easy targets.

"In, in, waste no time," Kanenas said, waving his little arms frantically.

Martala jumped in, followed by Alhazred. As I swung my leg over the lip of the well, the red gloom lit up with dazzling white.

Chapter Twenty-five

When I regained awareness, I thought I had been struck blind. All around was darkness. I felt hands touching my body, bearing me up, but for a time I could hear nothing. Then my ears began to ring and I heard their voices, faint and seemingly far away although they were touching me.

"Thank Baast," Martala said. "We thought you were dead."

"Did—" I had to stop and lick my lips. My mouth felt as though it had been packed with cotton. "Did the little man survive?"

"I'm here," Kanenas said. "The monster was aiming its blast at you."

"I was the bigger target," I said, which made him laugh in spite of himself. "Where are we?"

"In the tower, of course. Look up."

I did as Martala ordered and saw far above our heads a square of stars.

"Can it get through the well?"

"If it could, I suspect we would all be dead," Alhazred said.

They stayed with me, talking quietly in the darkness, until I was able to stand without swaying. My hearing slowly got better above the persistent ringing in my ears.

"I have heard stories of men who were struck by lightning and lived," Alhazred said. "I never fully credited them until now."

"It must have struck me in my side," I said, feeling my left ribs, and flexing my fingers. "And my right hand."

"Did you have your right hand on the rim of the well?"

Thinking about it, I nodded, then said aloud, "Yes."

"That is the path the lightning took through your body."

"If it had struck you fully, you would be dead," Kanenas said in a cheerful voice.

When they thought I was strong enough, we began our perilous descent down the dark stairs, which did not seem to be made for human feet. It was so easy to catch a heel on their edge and stumble. After I did so and almost fell off the edge, I moved with greater care. We went in single file, touching the person in front with the fingertips of one hand and the wall with the other. Alhazred took the lead and I followed with Kanenas behind me. Martala went last. She said little, and I realized her fury against Alhazred had not burnt itself out, but still smoldered inside her heart.

My own thoughts and emotions were divided at the course my teacher had chosen. He had sacrificed much to obtain this jewel. How could he flee from this world without seizing it, when it was sitting within his very grasp? And if what he said about Anisah was true, she had voluntarily sacrificed herself so that he could have it. I remembered seeing her nod, although the gesture had meant nothing to me at the time. Who was I to doubt her choice, as senseless as it might appear? Martala had evidently seen nothing. I wondered if Kanenas had noticed the gesture and wanted to question the little man, but could not speak about so thorny a topic in the presence of the Egyptian.

The descent seemed even longer than the ascent, if that were possible. It was also more tiring on my legs, which surprised me. I expected going down the stairs to be less laborious, but because the steps were not shaped for human legs, and because I could see nothing of them, it was harder due to the care I was forced to exercise.

I found myself laughing softly to myself, and realized I was still a little light-headed.

"What amuses you?" Kanenas asked behind me.

"I was just remembering the stories of adventure that were told to me in my childhood. In those tales, when the quest is completed, the hero always finds himself back home, or wherever else he wants to go, in a brief time and without trouble. But it seems that in real life, when you go forth on an adventure, the returning part is just as long and difficult as the going forth part."

"At least there aren't any hungry bats this time," Kanenas said.

"They weren't bats," I murmured, but did not pursue the issue.

At last we saw light far below. It began as a single point, and widened into a square that grew progressively larger as we descended. After what seemed an endless ordeal, I found myself standing in the great audience chamber of the house of the Shenghuo. It was eerily empty. The throne of the master was vacant.

"Are they lying in wait for us, do you suppose?" I asked the others.

"I doubt it," Kanenas said. "That is not their way. This may be the hour of their meditation, which they take together in the prayer hall. All the monks gather there once a day."

He swayed, and collapsed to the floor on one knee, then fell onto his face. I went forward with alarm and helped him to turn over. He blinked his eyes slowly.

"What's wrong with him?" Alhazred asked.

I looked up and shook my head.

"I don't know," Martala said. "He's never done this before."

"I need nourishment," the little man said weakly. "Opening that portal exhausted me. It's been so long since I lay in a fire."

"We can scarcely light an alchemical stove for you now," Alhazred said without emotion. "What can we get for you to eat?"

"Not eat, drink."

"Drink, then. Is there any wine in this place?"

"I don't need wine," Kanenas said weakly, looking at Alhazred.

"I think he wants blood," Martala said.

"Is that it? Will blood restore your strength?" Alhazred demanded.

Kanenas nodded.

"Give me your dagger," Alhazred said to Martala.

"You are still weak from your imprisonment. It should be me that feeds the creature."

He stood with his hand extended, meeting her gaze. At last she turned away, then turned back with the dagger in her hand. She passed it to him, and he used its edge to cut his arm above the wrist, then held the cut over the open mouth of the homunculus.

The first few drops of blood had a miraculous effect. Kanenas stirred. His eyes became clearer and focused on Alhazred's face. With eager hands he grasped the necromancer's arm and dragged it to his mouth. I saw his throat work and heard sucking sounds. Alhazred did not draw back, but let him drink his fill. Kanenas released his arm and stood easily.

"I am restored, for a time at least."

"Please tell us you can open a portal to our world," I said.

"This is your world," he said. "At least, it is partly in your world. Yes, I can open a portal, but not to Damascus. I must know the place where it will open, or it may open anywhere, as you already have experienced."

"We don't want it opening in the wilderness, or in the middle of the ocean," Alhazred said. "Can you take us back to the Soumela Monastery?"

"Of course."

"The black monks will kill us all," Martala said.

"What choice do we have? Even if we could find another portal to our world, we don't know where it would open. It might leave us on an island, or in a hostile land surrounded by foes. In any case, I very much doubt we would be able to find such a portal."

"Soumela it is, then," I said.

"I must prepare," Kanenas said. "It is more difficult than merely opening a door. There is distance through space to be considered, and various other factors."

"Don't explain to us how you do it," Alhazred said. "Just do it."

"We should leave this hall before the monks return. There is a room with a circle already inscribed on the floor. I have made many passages between the Plateau of Leng and the Soumela Monastery."

"Take us there."

He guided us through corridors and chambers, all of which were deserted. From some distant part of the monastery I heard a kind of droning that I recognized as the chanting of many voices. I wondered what use monks who cut off their tongues and sealed up their ears had for chants? It was not a mystery I intended to investigate.

The room where the portal was to be opened was completely empty and windowless. A single oil lamp burned in a wall bracket. In the dim light I was able to discern a complex circle that appeared to have been incised into the stones of the floor with chisels. These grooves were colored with a brownish-red pigment. I suddenly realized that it was dried blood.

"Will you need blood to open the portal?" I asked Kanenas.

He saw where I was looking and laughed at me. "That was done to consecrate the circle to Yog-Sothoth. It does not need to be repeated."

We stood back and watched him do his strange little dance inside the circle, while he muttered in some guttural language unknown to me.

"We must be ready for attack when we go through," Martala told Alhazred. "There are many black monks, all armed with swords and daggers. You have no weapon. Hassid has nothing except his mace and bone knife, which I fear will be of little use to him, and I have only my dagger."

"It is a chance we must take," he said. "We may be fortunate, as we were here. We may emerge in the monastery during the night when they are asleep."

"Perhaps Kanenas can control the hour when we emerge," she said.

"Do not break his concentration. We must take our chances and be ready for anything."

She nodded in agreement at Alhazred's words. I unwrapped my mace from around my waist, and hefted its stone in my hand. It was a poor weapon, but better than no weapon at all. I thought about offering it to my teacher so that he could defend himself, then reflected that I had practiced with it and he had not. It would be more effective in my hands. Instead, I drew the sharpened thighbone from my belt and extended it to him. Alhazred took it without comment.

The air began to shimmer above the pentacle incised into the floor. A dark oval formed. It floated just above the flagstones and was higher than my head by about a cubit.

"It is open," Kanenas said with a note of pride.

"Try to go through together," Alhazred said.

We gathered before it. Martala stood in front of Alhazred with her dagger drawn. I let the stone of my mace dangle on the end of its grass rope.

"Now!" Alhazred said.

We stepped forward together into the swirling oval vortex.

Chapter Twenty-Six

We returned, as I expected, into the same long chamber of pillars at the Soumela Monastery from which we had departed. I had lost reckoning of how many days ago that was. As we stepped forth, the portal shimmered for a few moments, then vanished. I looked around. It was impossible to tell in that windowless place whether it was day or night. Lamps burning on the walls gave enough illumination to see that the gallery was empty. No, not quite empty. At the far end, where the floor had been open there was now a heap of some kind. In the dim light it looked like a heap of discarded clothing.

"Eyes and ears open," Alhazred whispered. "Look for weapons."

We advanced down the gallery slowly, alert for any movement or sound, but the monastery was as silent as a tomb.

As we drew nearer to the pile of clothing, I saw bones sticking out from sleeves, and skulls half covered by black robes. They were reddened by blood, and there were patches of hair still clinging to some of them.

"There are swords," I muttered.

On top of the pile was a small, threadbare carpet. It was a moment before I recognized it as the carpet of Solomon. It rippled as if stirred by a wind, but there was no wind in the chamber. The air was dead and stank of rotting flesh.

With caution, I leaned inward and grasped the hilt of a

sword that projected from the pile of robes and bones. The carpet rippled and slid toward me. I jumped back with the sword before it touched me.

"Ly'saqua, lie still," Martala said in a commanding tone.

The carpet relaxed and lay motionless.

"What atrocity happened here?" Kanenas said in wonder, walking slowly around the heap of bloody bones.

Alhazred just shook his head, his eyes never leaving the carpet. "Is that what I think it is?"

"Kanenas says it is the flying carpet of King Solomon. To that I cannot testify, but it does fly after a fashion, and it did carry us here from Damascus," Martala said.

"It has a name?"

She nodded. "Your father obtained it for us; from where he did not say."

"You surprise me. I did not expect my father to involve himself in this affair. There are unwritten laws, and I have violated many of them."

"He could not search for you directly, but what he was able to do, he did. He is your father, Alhazred."

"Not all fathers care for their children, as you well know."

Each of us gathered weapons from the heap of the dead. There must have been the bones of dozens of men amid the blood-stained cassocks. I speculated that the carpet had stalked the monks through the rooms and corridors of the monastery, then dragged their corpses here to be consumed. I could think of no other reason why they should be heaped up in this way.

Kanenas could not manage a sword, but he took one of the smaller daggers and carried it before him with its blade thrust out. The blade was approximately the same length as his erect male organ, which was disproportionately large for his body. It was a sight I found disturbing.

With slow care we made our way through the monastery. It was deserted. All the monks either lay dead in the pillared gallery, or they had fled from whatever killed their brothers. From the state of uneaten food in the dining hall, it was evident that the slaughter had occurred many days before.

I was ready to declare the entire monastery empty when I heard a hushed voice behind a closed door. I motioned the others to come nearer and laid my hand on the panel with my sword at the ready. The latch would not move.

"Locked," I said.

Alhazred stepped up to the door and used the pommel of his sword to bang against it. "Whoever you are, you might as well come out. We won't hurt you."

There was no response. He hammered on the door a second time. "If you make us break this door down, we will be in a foul mood. I can't guarantee your well-being under those conditions."

I heard a soft voice speak from inside the room.

"What was that? Speak louder, I can't hear your words," Alhazred said.

"I said, is it gone?" It was a woman's voice.

I remembered the nuns at the monastery.

"It's the nuns," I told the others. "They must have fled in here to escape whatever killed the black monks."

The nun who had spoken repeated her question in a quavering voice.

"Is what gone?" Alhazred said in irritation. "Open this door so that we can talk properly. There is no danger out here."

After a few moments, the bolt rattled and the door opened a crack to show the frightened, tear-streaked face of a woman in her middle years. Alhazred gently but firmly pushed the door wide, and the woman, who wore a white nun's habit, shrank back to huddle with the other women in the small chamber, which was evidently used for storage of provisions for the table. I counted seven nuns.

"We are not going to harm you," Martala said in a gentle voice. She stepped through the door and held out her hand. "There's no danger. Come out with us."

At first they refused, but after the Egyptian coaxed them with soft words, at last they were induced to venture forth with terrified faces. They stared up and down the empty hallway, and seemed to relax when they saw nothing.

169

"Come with us into the dining hall, where we can sit and speak," Alhazred said.

"Are you quite certain that it has gone?" the elder nun asked.

"What has gone? What are you talking about?"

"The carpet, has it gone?"

"It is in the hall of pillars, but there is no danger," Martala said. "I command the carpet, and it is obedient to me."

The information that the carpet was still in the monastery roused their terror once again, but eventually Martala was able to persuade them to accompany us to the dining hall, where light shone in through the windows, allowing us to view their condition. Only one of them appeared to be injured, a young girl of no more than sixteen years who had a bloody gash on her left arm, which one of the other nuns had wrapped in a towel. Martala asked about the injury.

"It almost took Sister Anne," the older nun said. "We were able to pull her back and fight it off with brooms. The brothers were not so fortunate."

"Are you saying the carpet killed and ate all of the monks of the Order of Ambrose?"

"As to that, I cannot testify that it killed all of them. A few may have escaped down the mountain. But, yes, it killed most of them."

"And ate them?

She nodded.

Alhazred looked at Martala. "What is this thing that carried you from Damascus?"

"It never behaved in that way toward us," she said. "But we did see it seize and wrap itself around the Abbot Nicodemus. That was just before we stepped through the portal."

"It is a voracious monster," he said

"So it seems."

"Can you control it with its name?"

"I believe so. Your father assumed that we could, or he would never have provided it for our use."

"It is quite different from the tales I have read of Solomon's flying carpet."

She shrugged. "When a camel is given as a gift, it is uncourteous to examine its teeth. It has solved the problem of how to deal with the black monks."

"You speak truth. Can we trust it to bear us back to Damascus without eating us?"

"I believe we can. My knowledge of its name will restrain it. Besides, it must be replete to bursting with an excess of meat."

"I hope it's not too heavy to fly."

She explained to him that its manner of flight did not require it to lift above the ground.

"It's going to be crowded. We'll have to take the nuns away in additional flights," he said.

The elder nun overheard his words. "We are not leaving the monastery. This is our home. As long as you take that monster away with you, we will stay here."

The other nuns nodded.

Alhazred looked at Martala. "Very well, we can't make you leave. But there will be no brothers here to guard your safety or take care of you."

One of the nuns gave forth a harsh laugh and covered her lips with her fingers to stop herself. She blushed with embarrassment.

"Not having the brothers to protect us is the least of our worries, I assure you," the older nun said.

We left them in the dining hall and went to gather our packs from the room that had been assigned to us upon our arrival at the monastery. To my surprise, we found them where we had left them.

We discovered a hoard of gold dinars in the office of the Abbot Nicodemus, in his strong box. We took everything in the box and divided it between us. Alhazred carried Anisah's pack. Burdened in this way, we returned to the hall of pillars.

The carpet had not moved. Gingerly, Martala bent and reached out to grasp it by its edge. She backed away from the charnel pile and slid the carpet onto the stones of the floor. It lay motionless, looking like something any self-respecting householder would throw on the dung heap.

"Ly'saqua, we will mount upon you now. I order you to lie still," Martala said.

It was with a nervous heart that I huddled close to my two companions and moved with small steps onto the carpet. To my relief it lay quiet beneath my boots. I noticed that Kanenas stood some distance away, watching us with a solemn expression on his misshapen face.

"Get on," I told him. "There is enough room." I almost said, now that Anisah is gone, but stopped myself before the words escaped my lips.

"I am not going with you," he said.

For some strange reason, I felt disappointment at his words. I had grown accustomed to his presence, and could not deny that he was a useful traveling companion, given his ability to open portals.

"This is my home, or as much of a home as I have ever known." He pointed at the conical brick oven. "That alchemical furnace is my sleeping place. What would I do in Damascus?"

"It is your decision to make," Alhazred said with indifference.

"I have made it. Besides, were I to leave, who would take care of the nuns?"

My gaze strayed down to the enormous erection that jutted up from between his thighs. I held my tongue, keeping my unworthy thoughts to myself.

"We could not have succeeded in bringing Alhazred back to this world without your help," Martala told him. "We owe you a debt."

Kanenas nodded.

"Take good care of the nuns," Alhazred said.

"Ly'saqua, carry us back to Alhazred's courtyard in Damascus," Martala said.

Almost as quickly as she spoke the words, it was done.

Chapter Twenty-Seven

I jumped off the carpet as though its nap were burning the soles of my feet through my boots, and looked all around. We were back in Alhazred's courtyard beside the bubbling marble fountain with its glamour of flowing water. The eyes of the painted Greek statues looked down at us from their pedestals with mild amusement. Everything was as it had been when we left. I glanced up at the sun, and from its angle, judged it to be the middle of the morning. Birds sang in the fruit trees in the garden behind the house.

Alhazred approached me. "I believe you carry something that belongs to me."

For a moment I did not understand.

Sashi's beautiful face swam before my eyes. *Tell my beloved that I am ready,* she said in my mind. I repeated her words to my teacher.

He grasped my forearms with his hands, and greatly to my surprise, leaned forward and kissed me on the mouth. I felt something pass through my lips before I could pull my head away. I stepped back and wiped my mouth on my sleeve.

"Thank you for carrying Sashi," Alhazred said sincerely. "She could not have had a truer vessel."

I nodded, wondering if this should be taken as a compliment. That he had intended it as such, I had no doubt, but I thought of myself as more than a mere vessel.

Martala was carefully rolling up the carpet in a tight roll. She set her knee upon it and tied it securely, using several knots in each tie. "We must put this in a secure place," she murmured to Alhazred.

"And remember to feed it," he said.

"Your father will probably want it back in any case."

"He's welcome to it."

The brass-covered door of the house opened, and Brunni came out, rubbing his hands together. "I thought I heard voices. Welcome home, Master."

"It's good to see your face, Brunni," Alhazred said, and laughed. "Those are words I never would have believed I would ever say."

The servant looked puzzled, but nodded and smiled.

"Let us go into the front parlor where we can talk," Alhazred said to Martala.

"Is there anything to talk about?" she asked in a moody voice.

"There is."

I followed the two of them into the house, where servants took our packs.

"Bring wine," Alhazred told Brunni.

The three of us sat drinking red wine the manservant poured into our cups.

Martala waited until he left the room before speaking. "How are you going to tell Harkanos about his daughter?"

"I will tell him she voluntarily sacrificed herself so that I could fulfill my quest."

"Where is the jewel?"

He touched a place on his tunic.

"You should throw it away," she said with bitterness.

"If it were mine, I would do so."

"If it isn't yours, whose is it?"

He opened the front of his tunic and reached into its inner pocket. When he drew forth his hand, he held a small glass vial no larger than the end of his little finger. It contained a clear green liquid.

"It's for you."

She frowned and studied his face. "If this is a jest, it is a poor time for it. Where is the jewel?"

"This is the jewel, or rather, how the jewel presents itself in this reality."

"Why do you say it is for me? I don't want the cursed thing."

"You must take it. This is the true elixir of life about which so much nonsense has been written."

"You mean the elixir of the alchemists that is supposed to cure sickness and restore youth?"

"Precisely."

She sat and thought, watching him play with the little vial between his fingers. "I begin to understand," she said. "You didn't go on this quest for your own purposes; you went to secure this elixir for me, to restore my youth."

He shrugged. "I am half-djinn. I will live for centuries unless someone kills me first. How else are we to be together? You are growing old, Martala. I don't want you to die. I don't want to be alone in this world."

"You are a bastard!"

He blinked and raised his eyebrows at her fury. "Yes, I suppose I am."

"You let Anisah sacrifice herself, so that I could have a few more years of life?"

"So that we could continue to be together."

"Give me that vial, I want to smash it."

He closed his fingers around it and withdrew his hand. "We will talk again after you have rested and are more apt to listen to reason."

Whatever retort she intended was interrupted by Brunni, who entered and approached his master.

"What is it, Brunni?" he asked in irritation.

"A visitor, master. A young woman."

Alhazred looked at me, then at Martala. I shook my head to indicate I had no idea who it might be.

"This is not a good time, Brunni. We are all very tired."

"She was most insistent, master."

"Did she give a name?"

"She announced herself to be Anisah, daughter of our neighbor, Harkanos."

It is the only time I have ever seen my teacher struck speechless.

"It must be a trick of some kind, to get within our gates," Martala said. "The Old Ones must have followed us."

Alhazred shook his head slowly. "I don't think so. Show this woman into the house, Brunni. Bring her to me."

The cadaverous manservant bowed deeply and withdrew.

"I had hardly dared to hope," Alhazred muttered to himself.

"It must be a trick," Martala said, extending her dagger in her hand. She stood and positioned herself behind the door of the parlor.

A young woman wearing a bright yellow day dress and red leather slippers entered and stood looking at Alhazred, who had not moved from his chair.

"It is really you," I said in amazement, standing up.

"It is me, Hassid," she said with a smile. "Don't be afraid, Martala, it is truly Anisah."

Martala stepped from behind the door and walked around the girl, studying her in mute astonishment.

"How did you survive?" Alhazred asked quietly.

"The Dweller Beyond the Threshold took me as its sacrifice, but when it examined me, it decided that I was not amenable to its purposes and tried to dispose of me. I fought against it, and it cast me out of its world. By concentrating on my father's house, I was able to return here. I've been waiting for you all to get back."

"Thank Baast! You are unharmed," Martala said. She impulsively embraced Anisah. When she stepped away, there were tears of joy in on her cheeks.

"I sensed what I must do when we were in the tower chamber, and indicated to Alhazred that I was willing to become the sacrifice to the Dweller. But the god had not anticipated my strength, which came as much of a surprise to me as to it.

"I do not know how I fought it, only that I was able to

oppose its intentions. I think it grew fearful of me, and that it why it cast me from its world."

"I do not doubt that it was fearful," Alhazred said. "No one has ever had the power to oppose it."

"When you offered yourself to it, did you know you would be able to fight against it?" Martala asked.

"No, I only sensed that it was the right thing to do. I trust my instincts."

Martala looked uncertainly at Alhazred, and wiped a tear from her cheek with the back of her hand. "Did you know she would survive?"

Alhazred said nothing.

"Of course he knew," I said. "That's why he agreed to make the sacrifice."

"I will not stay longer," Anisah said. "You must all be tired from your long journey. I only wanted to assure you that I am alive and unharmed."

She turned and left the room. Brunni, who had hovered in the background while we spoke, escorted her out the front door and to the gate.

Martala stood staring hard at Alhazred. "You knew she would survive?" she asked again.

"I knew there was a chance that she would survive," he said.

"You truly are a bastard," she said in a soft voice.

He stood up and approached her, holding out the little vial of green liquid. "Take this. Unless you take it, everything I have done and everything you two did will be for nothing. What Anisah did will be for nothing."

Reluctantly, she accepted the vial and held it up to study it. "If you drank this, would it restore your face and manhood?"

"Drink it."

"Answer me, Alhazred."

"Probably. Yes, I believe it would do so."

"Then you should drink it." She offered it to him.

He stepped closer and put his hands on her shoulders, meeting her gaze with his.

"You are the most important thing in this world."

She trembled in his hands. I blushed and felt embarrassment to witness so intimate a moment between them, but there was nowhere I could withdraw without attracting attention to myself.

Her hands shook as she twisted out the glass stopper from the mouth of the vial. Blinking several times, she put the vial to her lips and tilted it in one quick motion. She closed her eyes.

Alhazred released her and stepped back.

A subtle change came over her. She began to glow with a soft, golden radiance that was like sunlight. The gray streaks in her hair vanished. Her face blurred, then cleared, and where there had been lines of age at the corners of her eyes and mouth, there was only smooth skin with a faint pinkness of new blood beneath it. When she spoke, her voice was stronger and clearer. "I'm not tired anymore. Do I look different, Alhazred?"

He looked at her for a long while in silence.

"You look like Martala once again," he said at last.

I marveled at the change. Where before a woman in her sixties had stood, there was now a girl no older than myself. She was beautiful.

Alhazred turned to me. There was a gentleness in his expression that I had never seen before. "Go home, Hassid. Your father will be delighted to learn that you have returned from your adventures unharmed."

I hesitated.

"What is it?" he asked.

"Master, now that you have come back to us, will you still be my teacher?"

He grunted. "Of course. I promised your father. Be here tomorrow at the usual hour for your next lesson."

I left them that way, standing silently, gazing into each other's eyes.

After all, what is the value in becoming a necromancer, unless you can cheat death? That is the whole point of the study. So I thought to myself as I stepped, gingerly and with great care, over the rolled carpet of Solomon which had been left just outside the front door.

About the Author

DONALD TYSON is the author of novels and short stories chronicling the adventures of the Arab necromancer Abdul Alhazred, legendary writer of the *Necronomicon*. A regular contributor of stories to the Lovecraftian horror anthology series *Black Wings*, edited by noted Lovecraft scholar S. T. Joshi, Tyson has also written numerous nonfiction books on all aspects of Western occultism, from black mirrors and Germanic runes to chaos magic and sexual alchemy. He lives with his wife, Jenny, in a renovated farmhouse on the island of Cape Breton, at the northern tip of the province of Nova Scotia, Canada.

About the Artist

Steeped in the enthralling fantasy and science-fiction illustrations of the 1960s, '70s, and '80s, artist and illustrator **K. L. TURNER** brings a bit of old-school painterly style to today's methods. With more than 30 years of experience in the arts, he expertly brings an expressionistic style into his illustrations to create compelling works which captivate and draw the viewer in. His works are found in media and galleries around the world, and celebrated in pop culture. A versatile creative type, Turner is accomplished in the mediums of photography, sculpture, and the fine arts.

Colophon

The text was set in Clavo Book.
Caliph, Harquil, Matura MT
Script, and qurban feast were
used for titling; Mohammed
was used for the drop caps; and
OldEgyptGlyphs for ornaments.